"Will you dance with me?"

Turning, Loris found herself looking into a lean, tanned face, with a straight nose, a cleft chin and a mouth that was firm, yet sensitive.

Again she got that illusory feeling of having once known him, a haunting sense of *recognition*, without being able to place him.

Her breath came faster, and it took a moment or two to steady herself. "I'd love to dance with you," she answered.

His hold light, but far from tentative, he steered her onto the dance floor. "I'm Jonathan Drummond." He volunteered no further information.

The name was unfamiliar. Though she was almost convinced they hadn't, she felt compelled to ask, "Have we ever met before?"

LEE WILKINSON lives with her husband in a three-hundred-year-old stone cottage in a Derbyshire village, which most winters gets cut off by snow. They both enjoy traveling and recently, joining forces with their daughter and son-in-law, spent a year going around the world "on a shoe-string" while their son looked after Kelly, their much-loved German shepherd dog. Her hobbies are reading and gardening and holding impromptu barbecues for her long-suffering family and friends.

Books by Lee Wilkinson

HARLEQUIN PRESENTS®
2154—SUBSTITUTE FIANCÉE
2183—THE DETERMINED HUSBAND

Lee Wilkinson

MARRIAGE ON THE AGENDA

HARLEQUIN®

TORONTO • NEW YORK • LONDON
AMSTERDAM • PARIS • SYDNEY • HAMBURG
STOCKHOLM • ATHENS • TOKYO • MILAN • MADRID
PRAGUE • WARSAW • BUDAPEST • AUCKLAND

ISBN 0-373-12228-4

MARRIAGE ON THE AGENDA

First North American Publication 2002.

Copyright © 2001 by Lee Wilkinson.

This edition published by arrangement with Harlequin Books S.A.

Visit us at www.eHarlequin.com

Printed in U.S.A.

CHAPTER ONE

THE taxi skirted Hyde Park and dropped Loris Bergman outside the Landseer Hotel. Having paid the driver, she hurried inside and crossed the plush lobby to the Ladies' Cloakroom.

When she had shaken the raindrops from her hooded cloak she gave that, and the small weekend case she was carrying, to the attendant, before glancing quickly in the mirror to check her image.

It was a bad enough crime to be so late for Bergman Longton's St Valentine's party, without her appearance being found wanting.

A small oval face with a pure bone structure, a wide, passionate mouth and almond-shaped eyes the colour of pale sherry, looked back at her. To others, her beauty was startling, but to Loris, with her total lack of vanity, familiarity had made her looks commonplace.

Satisfied that her long black hair and wispy fringe were tidy, and she looked cool and collected, she headed for the chandelier-lit ballroom.

The party was in full swing, with music and laughter and conversation. Some of the guests were dancing to a good-sized band, others milling about or gathered, glass in hand, in little groups.

A fair-haired, slimly built man, just under six feet tall and wearing impeccable evening dress, was standing alone in the background. His very stillness amongst the lively throng drew Loris's attention. She had a fleeting sense of familiarity, a feeling that a long time ago she might have known him.

A second look convinced her she was mistaken.

If she had ever met this man, with his look of maturity and quiet strength, his unmistakable air of self-assurance, she would have remembered.

His stance was easy, relaxed, back straight, feet a little apart. A slightly cynical expression on his good-looking face, he was watching the other guests.

She was wondering who he was, and what he was doing at the gathering, when his brilliant, heavy-lidded eyes met hers.

Suddenly meeting that cool, ironic regard had the same impact as walking into an invisible plate-glass window. A sense of shock made her stop in her tracks while her heart began to beat in slow, heavy thuds.

As she stood, momentarily held in thrall, her mother's voice said, 'So there you are, at last...'

Tearing her gaze away from the stranger's with an effort, Loris turned to the petite, dark-haired woman, whose still-beautiful face was marred by an irritable expression.

'We were beginning to wonder where on earth you'd got to. Your father's certainly not pleased.'

'I told you I had a six-thirty appointment and would no doubt be late,' Loris said patiently.

'It's utterly ridiculous on a Saturday night! And you didn't say you'd be *this* late. The party's more than half-over.'

Although her parents knew quite well that as an interior designer Loris frequently had to work unsociable hours, they always kicked up the same kind of fuss, treating her like a recalcitrant teenager rather than a confident, talented woman with a blossoming career.

'Unfortunately Mrs Chedwyne who is a client I can't afford to lose, wouldn't be hurried, and when I did manage to get away I still had to go back to the flat to change.'

Refusing to let the subject drop, Isobel Bergman complained, 'I don't know why you don't insist on people consulting you during normal business hours.'

Loris sighed. 'It doesn't work like that. I have to visit my clients' homes at *their* convenience. Quite a number of them are out during the day. Some only have weekends or evenings free.'

'Well, don't be surprised if Mark's furious. After all, it is a special party to celebrate the Cosby takeover, and it was your place to be by his side. He's missed you.'

Spotting her fiancé on the dance floor entangled with a tall, vivacious blonde, Loris remarked tartly, 'He doesn't appear to be missing me at the moment.'

'When you're this late what can you expect? You should have been here to keep an eye on him. If you're not careful some scheming little gold-digger will steal him from under your nose.'

Though Loris was well aware of Mark Longton's tendency to be attracted by a pretty face, the notion that she needed to 'keep an eye' on him wasn't a particularly pleasant one.

'Don't forget Mark Longton's quite a catch,' Isobel persisted. 'A handsome, sexy man, still in his thirties, who runs a company and has money, isn't to be sneezed at.'

'I'm not interested in his money,' Loris said flatly.

'Well, you ought to be. Your father's turned sixty, and if I can't get him to change his will when he dies your stepbrother will get the lot and you'll be left out in the cold...'

Simon, extrovert and loaded with charm, had always held pride of place in Peter Bergman's affections and, knowing what she did know, Loris hadn't been at all surprised by her father's decision. But well aware that it had been a bitter blow to Isobel to learn that her husband's son from his first marriage was to inherit everything, Loris said soothingly, 'I really don't mind if Simon does get the lot. I have a career I enjoy and—'

'It shouldn't be *necessary* for you to work. Your father could easily afford to give you an allowance—'

'I'm twenty-four, not fourteen.'

Ignoring her daughter's protest, Isobel rushed on, 'Seriously, I'd never have married him if I'd known he'd turn out to be such an old skinflint.'

It was a familiar complaint, and one that Loris had learned to studiously ignore.

'He's even talking about giving up the London flat and semi-retiring to Monkswood.'

'A lot of people work from home these days, and it would make it a lot easier to run the estate.'

'Well, I don't want to be stuck in the country the whole week. I'd go mad. But your father only thinks of himself, never of me. Weekends are bad enough—' Isobel continued to complain '—unless we're having a house party... By the way, I hope you remembered to bring some things?'

Loris and Mark were joining the weekend house party at Monkswood, the Bergmans' country estate which bordered on the village of Paddleham.

'Yes, I remembered.'

As the dance ended and the floor cleared, both women looked for Mark's tall, thickset figure, but he was nowhere to be seen.

'There's still plenty of food on the buffet if you want to eat?' Isobel suggested.

Loris shook her head. 'I had a sandwich before I went to keep my appointment.'

'Well, I could do with something. This latest diet is much too severe...'

At forty-seven, Isobel waged a continuous, and mainly losing, battle against the extra pounds that middle-age had piled onto her once-slim figure.

'And I'm convinced the pills they gave me with it are making my migraines worse,' she grumbled, as she disappeared in the direction of the buffet.

A waiter approached with a tray of champagne and, accepting a glass with a word of thanks, Loris sipped the well-chilled wine while her gaze travelled over the assembled company.

As she scanned the crowd, instead of Mark's heavy, slightly florid face, with its thick black brows and dark eyes, she found herself looking for a stranger's lean, tanned face, with clear-cut features and light, penetrating eyes.

A sudden fanfare called for the assembled company's attention, and Loris watched as her father, her fiancé, and a thin, balding man, went up onto the dais in front of the band. Sir Peter Bergman, stocky and tough-looking, with shrewd blue eyes and iron-grey hair, stepped forward and held up his hand for silence.

'Most of you already know that Bergman Longton and the American giant, Cosby, have been planning to amalgamate. I'm delighted to announce that that has now taken place, and William Grant—' he drew the thin, balding man forward '—one of Cosby's top executives, is here with us tonight to celebrate the event.'

There was a burst of applause.

'This merger will make us one of the largest and, we confidently expect, one of the most successful companies in our particular field. We have decided to rename the UK part of our combined companies BLC Electronics.' He raised his glass. 'May BLC go from strength to strength.'

There was more enthusiastic applause, and the toast was drunk.

As the three men left the dais they were momentarily swallowed up by a surge of people wanting to shake their hands and offer congratulations.

When the excitement had died down and the crowd began to disperse, Peter Bergman and William Grant walked away together, talking earnestly.

Mark glanced towards where Loris was standing, striking in an aquamarine dress that clung to her slender figure. She smiled and moved in his direction, but his face was cold, and he turned away to join the woman he'd been dancing with earlier.

Stunned by the rebuff, Loris stopped in her tracks. Admittedly she was very late, but she had warned Mark in advance that she might be.

Still, she felt a certain amount of guilt, and if it hadn't been for the blonde, who was laughing up at him, she would have gone over and apologised.

But uncertain of his reaction—Mark could be very unforgiving when something displeased him—she hesitated, having no wish to be humiliated in front of the other woman.

As she stood wondering how to retrieve the situation, a special St Valentine's waltz was announced. '...at the conclusion of which, gentlemen, you may kiss your partner.'

Surely Mark would come over to her now?

But without hesitation he offered his hand to the blonde.

Biting her lip, Loris was about to walk away, when a low, attractive voice, with just a trace of an American accent, asked, 'Will you dance with me?'

Turning, she found herself looking into a lean tanned face, with a straight nose, a cleft chin, and a mouth that was firm, yet sensitive. A very masculine mouth that sent tingles through her, a mouth she could only describe as beautiful.

Again she got that illusory feeling of having once known him, a haunting sense of *recognition*, without being able to place him.

His thickly lashed eyes, she saw at close quarters, were sea-green rather than the silvery-grey she had thought them to be. Their impact was just as devastating, making her pulses start to race and her breath come faster, so that it took a moment or two to steady herself.

Though part of her *wanted* to dance with this fascinating stranger, Loris was well aware that accepting his invitation would only serve to exacerbate things.

Despite the fact that Mark had a roving eye himself, since she'd agreed to marry him he'd proved to be both jealous and possessive, hating her to so much as look at any other male.

Bearing that in mind, she was seeking a polite way to refuse when, noting her hesitation, the man by her side asked sardonically, 'Scared that Longton won't approve?'

So he knew who they both were.

'Not at all,' Loris denied crisply. 'I…' She broke off as Mark and his partner circled past, close as Siamese twins.

Catching her companion's eyes, she saw the unspoken derision in their clear, green depths.

To hell with it! she thought with a spurt of anger. Why should she refuse? Mark had chosen to dance with someone else, and what was sauce for the gander…

She knew by now that if anyone failed to stand up to him he simply walked all over them and, though she hated any kind of discord, she had no intention of being a door-mat when they were married.

'I'd love to dance with you,' she finished firmly.

He smiled at her, a smile that lit his eyes and made little creases at each corner of his mouth. His teeth were excellent, white and healthy and gleaming.

She judged him to be around thirty years old and, wondering why such a relatively young, attractive man appeared to be here alone, she moved into his arms.

His hold light, but far from tentative, he steered her smoothly onto the floor. He was a good dancer, and they danced well together, their bodies fitting.

Mark, heavily built and well over six feet tall, dwarfed her slight five feet four inch frame, but this man was about six inches taller than herself, and her high heels brought their eyes almost on a level.

Meeting those brilliant eyes made her strangely breathless and, needing to say something, she remarked, 'You're aware that I'm engaged to Mark, so you must know who I am?'

'I do indeed. You're Loris Bergman.'

Something about the way he spoke made her say coolly, 'As I don't know your name, you have the advantage of me.'

'I'm Jonathan Drummond.' He volunteered no further information.

The name was unfamiliar. Though she was almost convinced they hadn't, she felt compelled to ask, 'Have we ever met before?'

'If we had, I would have remembered,' he replied.

'So how do you know me?' she asked curiously.

'Who doesn't?'

'Most of the people here, I imagine.'

He shook his head. 'I'm sure they all know the lucky woman who has one of the big bosses for a father and the other for a future husband.'

'You sound as if you disapprove?'

'It seems like an eminently suitable arrangement to keep all the money and power in the same family.'

'Money and power have nothing to do with it.'

'Really?'

'Yes, really.'

'Then why are you marrying Longton? Apart from the fact that he's a divorcé and much too old for you, he's not a particularly nice character.'

'Being a divorcé isn't a crime, and he's only thirty-nine.'

'I notice you haven't defended his character.'

'As that's only *your* opinion, it didn't seem necessary.'

'Neither have you answered my question.'

'We happen to love each other.'

At that moment Mark came into view. His partner's arms were round his neck, and he was saying something in her ear.

'He has a strange way of showing it.'

'I'm afraid he's angry with me for being late.'

'Has he any right to be?'

'Some, I suppose,' she answered honestly.

In response to Jonathan Drummond's raised brow, she briefly explained the circumstances.

Coolly, he said, 'As Longton was pre-warned, I don't see any justification for him behaving like a spoilt child. Do you?'

Challenged, without thinking how it might sound, she spoke the truth. 'Not really. That's why I'm dancing with you.'

'I see. Tit for tat. I guess it was too much to hope that you actually *wanted* to.'

As he finished speaking the dance ended, leaving Mark and his partner standing close by.

As couples began to kiss, Jonathan Drummond waited quietly, making no move.

Mark glanced in Loris's direction and, seeing that she was watching him, bent to kiss the blonde, who responded with enthusiasm.

Vexed by such deliberate provocation, Loris slid her palms beneath the lapels of her companion's dinner jacket and raised her face invitingly.

For a moment he stood perfectly still, then, taking her wrists, he lifted her hands away. 'I don't care to be *used*,' he said coldly.

'I-I'm sorry, she stammered, feeling cheap and foolish. 'I didn't mean—'

'Oh, I think you did. Goodnight, Miss Bergman.'

As she stood unhappily and watched him walk away, Isobel appeared by her side. 'Your father and I are leaving now.'

Loris pulled herself together and, knowing how her mother loved social occasions, asked, 'I thought the party went on until twelve?'

'It does, but it's almost eleven now, and with such heavy rain your father thought we should get started. Most of our guests came to Monkswood last night and are settled in, but one couple weren't due to arrive until this evening.'

Fretfully, she added, 'It's all a bit of a mess. If I'd realised earlier that this company party coincided with our house party I'd have done something about it. But by the time I discovered the muddle over dates it was too late and I—'

'Is Simon there?' Loris tried to stop the flow.

'No, he's staying in Oxford with some friends. I presume you'll be driving down with Mark as soon as the party's over?'

'I suppose so,' Loris said uncertainly.

'You mean he's still with that blonde creature? Yes, I see he is. She's probably after his money... Well, you've only got yourself to blame. All in all you've managed to make a real mess of the evening.'

'It's not entirely my fault,' Loris protested. 'If Mark had been a little more understanding...'

'When have men ever been understanding?'

'I'm sure *some* are.'

'Well, not the macho ones like Mark and your father.' Obviously wondering if she'd said too much, Isobel added hastily, 'Though who wants to be married to a wimp?'

'Not me.' For the first time that night, Loris smiled.

Peter Bergman thrust his way through the crowd and addressed his wife. 'About ready?'

'I only have to get my coat.'

Giving his daughter a look of extreme displeasure, he asked brusquely, 'I suppose you realise you've spoilt the entire evening? Have you any idea just how angry and disappointed Mark is?'

'He's made it quite plain,' she answered wearily.

'Then it's up to you to apologise. And as soon as possible.'

'Do,' Isobel urged as she prepared to follow her husband. 'Otherwise they'll both sulk for the rest of the weekend and it'll be murder.'

Loris was surprised by her mother's caustic observation. Though Isobel frequently criticised her husband, she had never been known to admit to even the slightest imperfection in her future son-in-law.

'You may well be right,' Loris admitted as she kissed the proffered cheek.

'I expect we'll be in bed before you get to Monkswood, so I'll see you in the morning. By the way, you and Mark have your usual rooms.' Isobel hurried away.

Knowing that the only possible chance of saving what was left of the weekend would be to get her apology over as quickly as possible, Loris began to look for her fiancé.

She finally spotted him standing, tall, dark, and powerful-looking, apparently bidding goodnight to some people who were leaving early.

Though he was still what most people would have called 'a fine figure of a man', she noted, with almost a feeling of betrayal, that his black, crinkly hair was showing signs of grey, his jawline had lost its firmness, and he had the beginnings of a paunch.

Relieved to find the blonde was nowhere in sight, she hurried over, and said quickly, 'Mark, I'm terribly sorry I was so late. I know you have every right to be angry with me, but please don't let it spoil the weekend.'

His brown eyes showing no signs of forgiveness, he snapped, 'The party's almost over. Isn't it a bit late for apologies?'

'I would have told you I was sorry straight away if you'd been alone.'

'Pamela's a beautiful woman, don't you think?'

When Loris said nothing, knowing he was just rubbing it in, he added, 'She comes from the States. Her father is Alan Gresham, the American newspaper magnate, which makes her heir to the Gresham millions.'

'How nice.'

So her mother was wrong. It wasn't Mark's money the blonde was after.

'She's made it quite obvious she fancies me.'

Loris's lips tightened in distaste. 'Don't you find her just a bit blatant?'

'She certainly knows her way around,' he said admiringly. 'And she's not the sort to say no, which makes a nice change.'

So it wasn't just her late arrival he was punishing her for. Her refusal to go to bed with him was a good part of it.

In the three months they had been engaged Mark had been fairly pressing, and several times, deciding she was being stupid in holding back, she had almost given in.

He was a handsome, virile man, and she had little doubt that he would make a good lover. Yet each time when it came to the crunch, perhaps still inhibited by the past, she had changed her mind.

Understandably, this had enraged Mark, who had sulked for days. He would be perfectly normal with everyone else, but only address her when he absolutely had to, and then be brief and glacial.

Reading the signs, Isobel had once said seriously, 'I know sleeping together is almost the norm these days, but

I think you're right to hold back until the wedding ring's on your finger.'

It was the first time her mother had ever broached the question of sex and, wondering if she had somehow guessed what had happened with Nigel, Loris had asked, 'Why do you say that?'

'Because Mark's the sort of man who, when he's got what he wants, might well lose interest and start to look elsewhere...'

Like Nigel.

'Of course once you're his wife it won't matter so much. After one divorce, I imagine he'll be fairly discreet.'

Profoundly disturbed by what her mother was suggesting, Loris had said, 'You sound as if you think he'll stray.'

'Don't most men? And I can't imagine a man like Mark being satisfied with one woman.'

Seeing her daughter's expression, Isobel had added, 'After all, what does it matter? You'll have money and position, a good lifestyle. Mark seems generous enough. Unlike your father.'

'I don't happen to want that kind of marriage,' Loris had said quietly.

'Well, of course I could be totally wrong.' Isobel had hastily backed off. 'Mark is getting to the age where he might be ready to settle for the faithful husband bit...'

Becoming aware that Mark was waiting for a response to something she hadn't heard, Loris said, 'Sorry?'

'I merely remarked that if you're jealous of Pamela, you know what to do about it.'

'But I'm not jealous,' Loris denied calmly.

Looking distinctly put out, Mark asked, 'Then why did you rope in that wimp to dance with you?'

'I didn't "rope him in". He asked me.' Remembering Jonathan Drummond's quiet self-assurance, his firm refusal to be used, she said, 'And I certainly wouldn't describe him as a wimp.'

Eyes narrowing, Mark queried, 'Had you met him before?'

'No.'

'Did he know who you were?'

'Yes.' Remembering his comments about Mark, she added, 'I gather you and he know each other.'

Mark looked down his nose. 'I'd hardly say *know*. I've seen him knocking around the offices.'

'Who is he?'

'Just some Johnny-come-lately. He's over from the States with the Cosby crowd.'

Of course. She recalled that his attractive voice had had a slight American accent.

'What does he do exactly?'

'No idea,' Mark said dismissively. 'He's sat in on most of the meetings, but I gather he's there in some minor capacity. Secretary or PA to one of the executives, or something of the sort. Why do you want to know?'

Unwisely, she admitted, 'I found him interesting.'

Looking at her as if she'd lost her senses, Mark echoed, '*Interesting*?'

'He seemed unusually cool and self-possessed. Very much his own man.'

Mark snorted. 'Though he had the infernal cheek to ask you to dance, I noticed he didn't have the nerve to kiss you.'

'I don't think it was lack of nerve.'

'Then he probably remembered his place.'

'Remembered his place?'

'Well, he's definitely not in our league.'

'I wasn't aware we had a league.' Her voice was as brittle as ice.

Sounding human for the first time, Mark said wryly, 'I thought you came over to apologise, not pick a quarrel.'

'I did. I'm sorry, Mark. Let's not talk about Jonathan Drummond.'

'Drummond, that's his name. I'll keep an eye on him from now on.'

'What do you mean by "keep an eye on him"?'

'Just that. It strikes me he could get too big for his boots.'

Well aware that Mark could be quite petty if he took a dislike to anyone, Loris wished she'd said nothing about Jonathan Drummond.

Wanting to change the subject, she asked lightly, 'So, now I've apologised for being late, are we friends again?'

Ignoring the question, he went off at a tangent. 'You do realise that when we're married you're going to have to give up this ridiculous job. I refuse to have my wife working all hours.'

'I won't be working all hours.'

'You are at the moment.'

'Only because I have to pay an exorbitant rent for my flat.'

'You could have gone on living at home.'

'I didn't want to.' Her desire to be independent had made her move as soon as she was able to support herself.

She made an effort to placate him. 'Once we're married the financial pressure will ease and I'll be able to choose just a few special clients.'

'When we're married you won't need *any* clients.'

'But I *want* to work.'

'I flatly refuse to let any wife of mine go about telling other people how to decorate their homes. It reflects badly on me. You must see that.'

'But what will I *do* all day?'

'Whatever it is that other rich men's wives do.'

Loris, who was about to argue, thought better of it. 'Well, I'm sure we don't need to discuss it just at the moment.'

'No, there are more important things to sort out.' He put an arm around her waist.

'Such as what?'

Bending his head, he said in her ear, 'I've had more than enough of your stalling. I want you to sleep with me tonight.'

'But we're at Monkswood.'

'All the rooms have a double bed. Either you come to me, or let me come to you.'

'No. I couldn't. Not in my parents' house.'

'Don't be an idiot, Loris. They need never know if you don't want them to. And even if we shared a room openly I know your father wouldn't mind. After all, we *are* going to be married. Oh, come on! You're living in the twenty-first century, not Victorian times.'

'Yes, I know, but I still don't feel comfortable about it.'

'Then come back to my flat with me now, and we'll go on to Monkswood afterwards.'

About to make the excuse that she wasn't in the right mood, she hesitated. Perhaps it *was* time she cut herself free from the past.

With today's sexual freedom there was little real justification for holding back, and Mark was clearly getting to the end of his patience.

She had opened her mouth to agree when he muttered angrily, 'Look, Loris, I'm warning you. This time I don't intend to take no for an answer.'

Hating to be pressured in this way, she felt her temper flare, and she snapped, 'I'm afraid you'll have to.'

Perhaps if he'd used his not inconsiderable charm, he might have succeeded in talking her round, but, in a mood for confrontation rather than conciliation, he threw down the gauntlet. 'Damn it, if you won't come back to my flat with me, I know someone who will.'

'I suppose you mean Pamela?'

His smile was an unpleasant combination of smugness and threat. 'She'll come like a shot, and I might just ask her.'

'Why don't you?' Loris said coldly, and, chin held high, stalked away.

Going to the Ladies' Cloakroom, she sat on one of the pink velvet chairs, staring blindly into the gilt-edged mirror while a trickle of women began to collect their coats.

The St Valentine's party was almost over, and as far as she was concerned the whole thing had been a total disaster. Had she known what trouble her being late would cause she would have cancelled her appointment, even if it had meant losing a client.

As it was, she'd displeased her father, made Jonathan Drummond think badly of her and, on this special night for lovers, thoroughly upset Mark.

Thinking of the promising moment that had suddenly metamorphosed into an unpleasant flare-up, she gave a deep sigh. Of course he wouldn't do as he'd threatened. The only reason he'd flaunted his conquest of the blonde had been to add weight to his demands, and his ultimatum had been caused by a build-up of anger that had needed to find an outlet.

But it was ironic to think that if it hadn't been for him jumping in too soon they would have been on their way to his flat by now. Perhaps, rather than reacting in the way she had, it would have been better if she'd controlled her temper and agreed to go, regardless.

Once they were lovers the tension between them would ease. They could go back to being happy and enjoying each other's company, rather than Mark, frustrated and resentful, quite often spoiling things by sulking.

She sighed deeply.

But it wasn't too late. She could always find him and apologise yet again. Tell him she'd changed her mind, she would go with him.

Joining a short queue, Loris collected her belongings.

Then, slipping her evening bag into one of the deep pockets of her cloak, she put the cloak over her arm and, case in hand, made her way into the crowded foyer.

She was scanning the throng for Mark when she noticed the blonde. Wearing an expensive-looking fur coat, Pamela was heading for the exit. As she reached it Mark, who had obviously been waiting for her, stepped into view. An arm around her waist, he escorted her through the heavy glass doors.

For a second or two Loris was shocked into stillness, then, a combination of anger and dismay making her heart beat faster, she pushed her way outside.

It was still raining hard, and she was just in time to see, through the downpour, Mark's silver Mercedes spray water from beneath its wheels as it pulled away from the entrance.

A gusty wind was driving icy rain beneath the hotel's brown and gold canopy but, oblivious to the cold and wet, she stood as if stunned, staring after the car.

'Suppose you put this on before you get saturated?'

Taking her cloak, Jonathan Drummond placed it around her shoulders and pulled the big, loose hood over her dark hair.

He himself was bare-headed, wearing only a short car-coat with the collar turned up.

'Let me have this.' He relieved her of the case.

'Thank you,' she mumbled. Then, unencumbered, began to walk towards a line of waiting taxis drawn up on the forecourt.

Reading her intention, he stopped her. 'I'm afraid you'll find they're all prebooked.'

'Oh,' she said blankly.

Putting his free hand beneath her elbow, he urged her towards a modest white Ford saloon. 'Jump in and I'll drive you home.'

CHAPTER TWO

STILL feeling stunned, Loris found herself being helped into the passenger seat. Her case was tossed in the back, and a moment later Jonathan Drummond slid in beside her.

She had made no move to fasten her seat belt, and he leaned over and fastened it for her. His fair hair was darkened by the wet and, feeling curiously detached, she watched a drop of water trickle down his lean cheek.

As they joined a queue of cars and taxis that were leaving the hotel forecourt and slowly filtering into the stream of late-night traffic, he said, 'You live in Chelsea, I believe?'

Loris pushed back her hood and, making an effort to come to grips with the situation, answered, 'That's right. But I wasn't intending to go to my flat.'

'Whose flat *were* you intending to go to?'

She bit her lip, and stayed silent.

Slanting her a glance, he murmured, 'I see. But you were unexpectedly...shall we say...replaced?'

So he'd seen Mark and the blonde driving away.

Gathering together the tatters of her pride, Loris informed him haughtily, 'I was intending to go down to my parents' house.'

'At Paddleham?'

Wondering how he knew so much, she answered, 'Yes.'

'So Longton was supposed to be going too?'

He was too quick by half. Sounding suitably amazed, she asked, 'How on earth did you deduce that, Holmes?'

Grinning, he answered, 'Elementary, my dear Watson. You didn't go with your parents, you don't have a car, and

23

you hadn't ordered a taxi. Which means you were expecting your fiancé to drive you down.'

Then, sounding as though he cared, 'No wonder you looked shattered, being treated so shabbily.'

'It was partly my own fault,' she admitted.

'All the same, it must hurt like hell.'

She said, 'I'm more angry than hurt.' And discovered it was the truth.

'Stay that way. Anger is easier to cope with.'

As they neared the head of the queue, he asked, 'So which is it to be? Chelsea, or Paddleham?'

'I can't ask you to drive me all the way to Paddleham,' she demurred.

'I'll be happy to, if that's where you want to go?'

'It isn't really,' she confessed, dismayed by the thought of having to try and explain Mark's absence. 'But I can't go back to my flat.'

'Gee that's tough, doll.' Sounding like a gangster in a second-rate movie, he asked out of the corner of his mouth, 'So what are the Mob after you for?'

She laughed in spite of herself.

'It's not quite that bad. I agreed to let an old college friend of mine have my flat for tonight and tomorrow night.'

'And there's only one bedroom?'

'Worse. Judy and Paul are on their honeymoon… Monday, they're flying to Oz to go backpacking.'

'Hmm… Well, if you can't go back to your flat and you don't want to go to Paddleham—' he gave her a villainous leer '—what about my place?'

Loris was about to curtly refuse, when she realised he was pulling her leg.

Lightly, she said, 'I'm afraid I'm superstitious about going anywhere new on a wet Saturday.'

'Pity.'

'But thanks all the same.'

'Think nothing of it. We aim to please. So what's it to be?'

Briefly she considered asking him to take her to a hotel, then dismissed the idea. She could well do without the expense. In any case, by breakfast-time next day her parents would require some kind of explanation. Though she dreaded the prospect, her practical streak insisted that it would make sense to be there in person to make it.

Coming to a decision, she said, 'If you really don't mind, I think I'd better go to Paddleham.'

'Paddleham it is.'

A moment or two later they had joined the traffic stream and were heading out of town through gleaming, rain-lashed streets.

Worrying her bottom lip, she wondered how she was going to explain away Mark's absence.

Of course she could simply tell her parents the truth. But if she did she knew it would be *her* they would be blaming, saying she'd brought it on herself.

Which in a way she had. If she hadn't been late for the party in the first place. Though her lateness, she recognised, had only been the catalyst. None of this would have happened if she'd agreed to sleep with Mark when he'd first pressed her to.

But, even after six years, the remembrance of the shame and humiliation she had suffered over Nigel was still a powerful deterrent.

She had been in her first year at art school when she had met him. The son of Sir Denzyl Roberts, one of her father's wealthy friends, Nigel had been five years older, and light years ahead of her in experience. Expecting her to be like most of the women he had known, he had been surprised and intrigued to find she was supremely innocent.

On her part it had never been a conscious decision to

remain a virgin. It had just happened. Since her early teens her unusual beauty had made her a target for every male aged between fifteen and fifty. But, naturally fastidious, she had kept them at bay, disliking their one-track minds and fly-paper hands. Waiting for someone special. Someone she could love.

There had been one boy, different from the rest, a fleeting attraction that might have developed into something deeper if, before she could get to know him, he hadn't vanished from the scene.

At the same time she had met Nigel. Impressed by his looks and maturity, and perhaps falling in love with love, she had fondly imagined *he* was that someone special.

Even so, almost out of force of habit, she had held him off until, rapidly losing patience, he had proposed to her.

Though she had still been very young, the match, from her parents' point of view, had been an advantageous one and, highly delighted, they had encouraged the engagement.

Once the ring was on her finger, Nigel had redoubled his efforts to get her into bed. Certain she loved him, and happy in the knowledge that they were going to be married, she had given in.

Loris had found their lovemaking disappointing, getting little or nothing from it. She had consoled herself with the thought that it was bound to get better when they were used to each other.

It hadn't.

Blaming herself, her inexperience, she had said nothing, merely kept on trying to please him.

They had been sleeping together for almost three months when, turning up unexpectedly at his flat one evening, intending to surprise him, she had found him with another woman.

Though hurt and bewildered, she had been ready to forgive him, until the girl in his bed had taunted her with the fact that this was no one-off, but was, and had been for some time, a regular arrangement for the nights Loris wasn't there.

'He needs a woman who's got some life in her, who knows how to please a man. Not some frigid statue who just lies there and—'

'That's enough!' Nigel had silenced her at that point.

But it had been too late. As far as Loris was concerned, the damage had been done. Nigel had told this brazen slut of a girl intimate details about something she had considered essentially private and sacrosanct.

Badly humiliated, and furious at the way he had treated her, she had thrown his ring at him and walked out.

When her father and mother had learnt of the broken engagement, deploring the fact that she was 'losing her chance to marry well', they had tried to get her to change her mind. But, while refusing to tell them the reason for the break-up, she had made it clear that it was final.

Judy, her friend and room-mate at college, was the only one in whom she had confided her hurt, but down-to-earth as usual, Judy had pulled no punches. 'Think about it. Would you really *want* to marry a two-timing rat like that?'

'No, I suppose not.'

'Then forget him. He's not worth a second thought.'

'I just wish I hadn't been such a fool.'

'Well, we all make mistakes. It isn't the end of the world.'

It had only felt like it.

'I thought he loved me,' Loris had said sadly. 'But he was only *using* me.'

'Surely you got something out of it?'

Loris had shaken her head wordlessly.

Judy had said a rude word. 'Still, it'll be different next time, you'll see.'

But, feeling degraded by the experience, Loris had

vowed there would *be* no next time. Even so, it had taken her a long while to regain her self-respect...

Flashing lights suddenly reflected in a myriad raindrops, and the urgent sound of a siren bearing down on them brought Loris back to the present with a start.

The road they were on was narrow, and there was on-coming traffic. Pulling half-onto the wet, deserted pavement, Jonathan made room, and a second later the ambulance went racing past on its errand of mercy.

Impressed by his presence of mind, she glanced at him. His face was calm, unperturbed.

Intercepting her glance, he gave her a sidelong smile that quickened her pulse-rate and made her feel suddenly breathless.

A moment later they had regained the road and were continuing their journey. By now they were on the outskirts of town, and the downpour was continuing unabated. Rain beat against the windscreen and even at their fastest speed the wipers had a job to keep it clear.

As they reached a crossroads and turned right it occurred to Loris, belatedly, that she had given him no directions and he had asked for none.

Wondering how, being from the States, he knew the way, she queried, 'Are you familiar with this part of the world?'

'I was born and brought up quite near Paddleham.'

'Really? Then your parents were English?'

'My father, a hard-working GP, was English while my mother, who was an airline stewardess until she married, came from Albany.'

'The capital of New York State?'

'That's right. Her parents owned a small business there.'

To Loris, the details of his modest background seemed at odds with his cultured voice.

'Have you lived in the US long?' she asked, wanting to know more about him.

'For several years now.'

She thought he was going to leave it at that, when he added, 'After my father died my mother got homesick for her birthplace and went back to Albany.'

'Do you have any brothers or sisters?'

'One sister. When she left university she married the son of a local landowner. But there was nothing to keep me here, so I spent some time travelling, trying my hand at various jobs, before I made up my mind to settle in the States.'

His answers had been easy enough, but when he volunteered no further information, afraid of sounding nosy, she relapsed into silence.

Once the suburbs had been left behind them, from being unpleasant, the journey became positively hazardous. The country roads were dark and muddy, littered with snapped-off branches and storm debris.

In the bright tunnel made by their headlights Loris could see that a lot of the verges were partially flooded, and though Jonathan drove with care their nearside wheels almost constantly threw up a wave of water.

Just before they reached their destination a swollen stream that had overflowed its banks, and covered the low-lying road to what he estimated was an unnavigable depth, made a detour necessary. Feeling guilty at having dragged him so far on such a terrible night, Loris was seriously wishing she had plumped for a hotel.

'I'm sorry about all this,' she apologised.

Sounding quite unconcerned, he said, 'You mean the conditions? Don't worry—I've driven in a great deal worse.'

A few more minutes and they were passing through the dark and sleeping village of Paddleham. An occasional streetlamp lit up the driving rain, and strung high across the roadway a saturated banner announcing a St Valentine's dance at the village hall flapped dementedly in the wind.

The Yew Tree came into sight, its inn sign swinging on the supporting chains. 'We're almost there,' Loris said, making no attempt to hide her relief. 'Just past the church there's a turning off to the left, then about half a mile down the lane, also on the left, you'll see the entrance to Monkswood. The gates should be open.'

The black and gold wrought-iron gates were open wide, and the Tarmacked drive was well-lit. Several sleek cars were parked on the paved apron in front of the house.

Jonathan drew up beneath the ornate lantern that hung over the porticoed entrance and, leaving the engine running, came round to help Loris out.

She couldn't fail to notice that, parked between a Porsche and a Mercedes, the ordinary little car looked out of place.

Key in hand, she had opened the door by the time he had retrieved her case. A chandelier in the hall, and one at the top of the grand staircase, had been left on, but the rest of the house was dark and still.

'I can't thank you enough for bringing me,' she said, as he handed over her case.

'It was my pleasure.' Briskly, he added, 'Well, everyone seems to be in bed, so I'll say goodnight and let you join them.'

As though her subconscious had already decided, she found herself saying, 'Please, won't you stay? I'd hate to think of you having to drive all the way back to town on a night like this.'

'I wouldn't want to put you to so much trouble.'

'It's the very least I can do. And it really is no trouble. Do stay. You can have Mark's room.'

Though he never moved a muscle, Loris sensed his surprise. Obviously he'd presumed that she and Mark shared a room.

'In that case I'll be happy to.'

Crossing to the car, he switched off the engine and doused the lights before joining her in the hall and relieving her of her case once more.

When she had closed the door behind him, and shot the heavy bolts, she turned and led the way up the richly carpeted stairs and through a decorative archway to the right.

'This is my room.' Taking her case from him, she put it inside before crossing the wide corridor to open a door opposite. 'And this is Mark's.'

Switching on the lights, she led the way into a comfortably furnished bedroom decorated in masculine colours of blue and grey.

'He doesn't leave clothes here, so I'm afraid I can't offer you any pyjamas.'

'That's all right.' Jonathan smiled. 'I don't use them.'

Feeling her colour rise, she said hastily, 'But you should find a new toothbrush and everything else you need in the bathroom cabinet.'

'Thank you.'

A thought struck her, and she added regretfully, 'Except a shaver, that is. I'm sorry.'

He shrugged. 'Don't worry. Though I can't see myself with a beard, in an emergency I have been known to wear designer stubble.'

'Well, goodnight.'

'Goodnight, Loris,' he said gravely.

Feeling curiously restless and unsettled, she went back to her own room and was about to prepare for bed when she thought of her stepbrother.

Though Monkswood was virtually Simon's second home, he wasn't going to be here this weekend. Consequently, in his bathroom, there would almost certainly be a razor that their last-minute guest could borrow.

Without further ado she hastened barefoot along the

darkened corridor to Simon's room and went in quietly.
Sure enough, on the bathroom shelf was an electric razor.
If Jonathan Drummond hadn't already gone to bed, she
could give it to him now, ready for the morning.

As she reached his room she saw through the multicol-
oured fanlight above the door that his light was still on.
Bearing in mind that not too far away people were sleeping,
she tapped softly. When there was no answer, she tried
again. Still no answer.

Perhaps he was in the bathroom?

She opened the door a crack, and could just make out
the sound of the shower running. Deciding to leave the
razor where he couldn't fail to notice it, she slipped inside
and tiptoed across the room to put it on the bedside cabinet.

Turning back to the door, she gave a half-stifled gasp.
Just emerging from the bathroom, Jonathan was in the act
of pulling on a short white towelling robe. His hair was
wet and rumpled, and drops of water still clung to the fine
golden fuzz on his legs.

Without undue haste or self-consciousness, he adjusted
the robe and fastened the belt.

Thrown by how irresistibly sexy he looked, and feeling
a sudden potent attraction, she stammered, 'I—I did knock,
but you must have been in the shower. I've brought you
Simon's razor. He won't be wanting it this weekend.'

A well-marked brow rose. 'Simon?'

'My stepbrother.'

'Ah, yes…'

Embarrassed to realise she was still standing goggling at
him like a fool, Loris prepared to make her escape. Only
to find that, somehow, Jonathan was between her and the
door.

'I'll say goodnight again.' She was aware that she
sounded breathless.

He took her hand, while green eyes smiled into gold.

Wits scattered, she stood gazing back at him like someone mesmerised, before making an effort to free her hand.

When he failed to release it, she said huskily, 'I must go.'

'Must you?'

Without realising how provocative it looked, she used the tip of her tongue to moisten lips gone suddenly dry.

Using the hand he was holding to draw her closer, he said softly, 'This time I think I'll take you up on the invitation.'

His free hand slid under the fall of dark silky hair to cup the back of her head, and a second later his mouth was covering hers.

Loris found his light kiss both pleasurable and exciting. But though it sent a tingle right down to her toes there was nothing alarming about it, nothing to warn her that she was in any danger.

While part of her mind pointed out that she shouldn't be letting this happen, another part answered that, as kisses went, it was relatively innocent.

She wasn't caught up, wasn't *involved*... She could walk away whenever she pleased.

But she hadn't reckoned on the seductive sweetness that, almost without her realising it, made her want the kiss to go on, made her want to kiss him back.

As her lips parted, his tongue-tip stroked along the velvety-smooth inner skin, making her quiver, before he deepened the kiss.

Mark's kisses were ardent, hot-blooded, sometimes bruising in their intensity. They totally lacked the finesse, the subtlety and imagination of this man's lovemaking.

He explored her mouth with a kind of delicate enjoyment that sent little shudders running through her, while, almost unnoticed, his free hand traced her slender curves.

When it found the soft swell of her breast and his thumb

brushed coaxingly over the nipple, she knew it was time to call a halt.

But the sensations that the thistledown-touch was arousing were so exquisite that every bone in her body seemed to melt, and an awakening hunger that refused to be stilled cried out for more.

Responding to that hunger, his lovemaking gradually became more intense as he added a new and disturbing dimension.

Passion.

But it wasn't a tempestuous, uncontrolled passion that might have swamped any response, or served to scare her. This was a leashed passion that lured her onwards, that enticed and invited an answering passion, until suddenly she was lost. Mindless. Carried away. Caught and held in a web of sensual delight...

Loris stirred and surfaced slowly from a deep and contented sleep, to find grey morning light was filtering into the room.

Though her mind was still enshrouded in a kind of golden haze, she was dimly aware that her body felt relaxed and satisfied.

She was stretching luxuriously when one of her feet brushed against a man's hair-roughened leg.

Shock hit her, and she stiffened as the sharp, cold wind of memory blew in, dispersing the haze.

Oh, dear heaven, what had she done?

After putting off her own fiancé for several months she had gone to bed with a virtual stranger.

She only just stopped herself groaning aloud.

Lying unnaturally still, afraid to move a finger, she listened to Jonathan Drummond's quiet, even breathing.

Satisfied that he wasn't yet awake, she turned her head slowly to look at him.

He was lying facing her, so close that they were almost

touching. His tanned skin was clear and healthy, his breath sweet. There were grooves each side of his mouth, and little laughter-lines radiated from the corners of his eyes. Thick, gold-tipped lashes lay like a fan on his high cheekbones.

It was the face she remembered from the previous night, yet not the same.

The mature self-assurance and the somewhat disturbing irony were gone from it. With his tousled hair and his confident mouth relaxed in sleep he looked endearingly boyish, in spite of the morning stubble adorning his chin.

But there had been nothing remotely boyish about him last night. His lovemaking had proved him to be a skilful and experienced man.

Heat ran through her as she remembered all the things he had made her feel, and her own unexpectedly passionate response. After the fiasco with Nigel, she had started to wonder uneasily if she might be frigid. That had been one of the reasons she had remained celibate for so long. She had been afraid to start another relationship in case the same thing happened.

But last night had proved that she could be warm and responsive and far from frigid. The fault hadn't been hers.

Nigel, she knew now, had been a selfish, uncaring, inept lover who, as well as mangling her self-respect, had almost destroyed her faith in herself as a woman.

Jonathan's skill and generosity, his imaginative love-making, had triggered a response that had shaken her to the core. For the first time in her life she had experienced all the joy and delight she had only ever dreamt about.

If it had been Mark she had spent the night with, she would be on top of the world.

Only it hadn't been Mark.

Rather than her own fiancé, it had been a man she had only just met. A man who would no doubt consider her *easy* and, in the cold light of day, feel nothing but contempt for her.

Gathering her wits, and desperate to get away before he awoke, Loris turned carefully onto her side. Her back to him, she was about to ease herself towards the edge of the bed when she felt him stir.

His arm came around her, and with a sleepy murmur of contentment he moved his warm palm to cup her breast.

Like some terrified animal, she froze into utter stillness, her heart pounding. She could feel the heat from his body, and his light breath stirring her hair.

After a moment or two his breathing returned to the evenness of sleep, the arm across her grew heavier, and she felt his hand relax its hold.

Taking a deep breath, she moved cautiously onto her back. Slowly, and with the greatest care, she eased herself from beneath the surprisingly muscular arm and slipped out of bed.

Though on one level she had *known* she was bare, the sight of her nakedness in the full-length mirror made her cringe. She averted her eyes.

The sooner she had put something on and was out of here the better.

Her last night's clothes were lying in an abandoned heap, one silk stocking trailing seductively.

She was reaching for her undies when a movement in the corridor outside brought her heart into her mouth. People were up and stirring, making their way down for breakfast.

Suppose one of the guests saw her creeping from room to room, still wearing what was obviously a party dress?

The towelling robe Jonathan had worn the previous night was tossed over a chair. Snatching it up, she pulled it on and fastened the belt. A quick glance at the bed, meant to reassure herself that he was still fast asleep, gave her a fresh shock. His green eyes brilliant, he was lying quietly watching her.

Gathering up her belongings, she fled without a word. Her timing couldn't have been worse. Just outside the door she ran slap into her father.

'So you did make it.' He didn't sound particularly pleased. 'I thought you might have changed your mind about coming. Our journey here was bad enough, and conditions were deteriorating fast.'

If only she had known how things were going to turn out, Loris thought vainly, she could have used the weather as an excuse for not being there...

Eyeing the tell-tale clothes she was clutching, her father added drily, 'Mark having a lie-in?'

She was saved from having to answer by a female voice cooing, 'Oh, *good morning*, Sir Peter.'

A red-haired overdressed woman she had never seen before was heading towards them.

Always a ladies' man, her father assumed an expression of charm. 'Good morning, Mrs Delacost. So sorry we weren't here to welcome you last night.'

'That's quite all right, Sir Peter. We didn't get back from Monte Carlo until quite late, and your wife *did* explain about the company's party...'

As she spoke, the redhead glanced curiously in Loris's direction.

Noting that look, Peter said without warmth, 'This is my daughter, Loris.'

Seeing her chance, Loris murmured a hasty, 'Good morning,' and bolted into her room.

As the pair moved away she could hear Mrs Delacost gushing, 'It was *so* nice of you to invite us to your lovely home...'

All of a tremble, Loris sank down on the nearest chair

and, twisting the magnificent half-hoop of diamonds she wore round and round her finger, gave a groan of despair.

Her father had been all for the engagement, encouraging it in every way possible, and she sensed that he had been far from displeased to find her leaving Mark's room. But when he discovered that Mark wasn't here it would be a very different story. He was likely to be livid, and that was putting it mildly.

She felt a leaden weight in the pit of her stomach.

Though he had never so much as raised his hand to her, preferring an icy silence or a cold reprimand when she displeased him, Loris had always shrunk from his anger.

But she was a twenty-four-year-old woman and independent, she reminded herself, not some schoolgirl. He had no right to tell her what or what not to do. No right to complain about her actions…

Except that it was his house. The last place she would have chosen to go off the rails and humiliate herself.

And that was exactly what she had done. It had been a stupid mistake. A one-night stand with no feelings on either side. She had been mentally condemning Mark, but she was no better. The only difference was that Mark's decision to sleep with someone else had been premeditated. Whereas hers had been anything but.

So where did that leave her engagement?

In trouble.

With the beginnings of a headache, she longed for a cup of coffee but, resisting the temptation to ring for some and linger over it, she went through to the bathroom to shower.

She would have to show her face and give some kind of explanation sooner or later, so better to get it over with. Though what explanation could she give for spending the night with a virtual stranger? She couldn't even explain to herself what had made her behave so out of character.

But perhaps it was better not to try and explain anything.

Merely give the bare facts and then relieve them of her company, even if it meant staying at a hotel.

Having made the decision, she was starting to feel a shade better when it occurred to her that she couldn't get back to London unless she left with Jonathan Drummond.

No! That wasn't an option. She would sooner call a taxi. The thought of driving all that way with the man who had seduced her was insupportable. Not that she hadn't been a willing victim, honesty forced her to admit. The blame was hers as much as his.

Belatedly it occurred to her to wonder how *he* was feeling. His behaviour hadn't been exactly praiseworthy.

Possibly, depending on what kind of man he was, he would be embarrassed by what had happened? Maybe he'd be as anxious to leave as she was to have him go? He'd been wide awake when she had left his room, so with a bit of luck he would just dress and slip quietly away.

When she had dried herself, she made-up lightly to hide an unusual paleness before dressing in fine wool trousers the colour of tobacco, a cream blouse, and an embroidered waistcoat. Then, summoning up every ounce of composure she could muster, she lifted her chin and sallied forth.

Drawn like a magnet to the door of the room opposite, she stood listening. Not a sound. Did that mean he'd already gone? She fervently hoped so. Shamed and mortified by her own weakness, she dreaded the thought of having to meet him face to face again.

And there was another consideration. An important one. If he'd gone without anyone seeing him she wouldn't have to divulge exactly *who* had slept in Mark's room. That would save trouble all round. Though she had no reason to try and *protect* Jonathan Drummond, if Mark and her father were to learn his identity it could cost him dear. They would, she felt sure, pressure Cosby's into getting rid of him on one pretext or another.

Needing to know for sure, she opened the door quietly and, holding her breath, peered inside. The room was blessedly empty, and the bathroom door, standing ajar, showed that was too.

Going over to the window, which overlooked the apron and the smooth green lawns at the front of the house, she peered out.

The rain had temporarily ceased, though the sky was heavy and overcast, threatening more. The garden looked battered and waterlogged, and shallow pools of water had gathered on the apron.

All the other sleek cars were still standing where they had been the previous night, but she could see no sign of the white saloon that Jonathan had been driving.

He must have gone back to London.

Sighing her relief, she made her way downstairs to the breakfast-room.

CHAPTER THREE

In the big, east-facing room all the lights were burning to counteract the dullness of the day. A few of the guests were still eating a late breakfast, while others lingered to converse over coffee, or glance through the Sunday papers.

There was no sign of her father, for which Loris was truly thankful. Though she recognised that it was cowardly, her impulse was to delay any showdown for as long as possible.

With a general, 'Good morning,' to the assembled company, she made her way to the end of the long table, where she froze in her tracks.

Sitting buttering toast and talking to her mother as though it was the most natural thing in the world, was Jonathan Drummond.

Fair hair smoothly brushed and shining under the lights, white teeth gleaming as he smiled in response to something Isobel had said, he looked infuriatingly attractive.

Glancing up, he saw her, and rose to his feet politely. 'Good morning.'

He was dressed in a pair of charcoal trousers, a pale-green shirt and matching tie, and a jacket she recognised as Simon's.

To her chagrin, he appeared cool and assured, every inch master of the situation.

Feeling the hot, embarrassed colour rising in her cheeks, somehow she answered, 'Good morning.' Then raggedly, 'I thought you'd gone.'

'Oh?' He came around the end of the table and pulled out a chair for her.

Sinking into it, she said almost accusingly, 'Your car wasn't there.'

'As I'd left it right in front of the entrance, I thought I'd better move it.'

Returning to his seat, and reaching for the marmalade, he added innocently, 'Your mother suggested that as it was a hired car it might be better in one of the garages.'

To get it out of sight, no doubt, as it lowered the tone. The words were unspoken, but the sardonic twist to his lips said it all.

Refilling his coffee cup, Isobel smiled at him, the perfect hostess, making it clear that, though his car might not be up to scratch, she found him very personable.

To Loris, she said expansively, 'Jonathan tells me he's with Cosby's…'

Wondering if her mother knew he was just a lowly PA, and deciding that she obviously didn't, Loris said nothing.

'I thought I remembered him from Ascot or somewhere, but obviously I was wrong…'

Ignoring the dishes keeping warm on the sideboard, Loris poured herself some coffee and drank it gratefully while her mother pursued, 'I've just been saying how very kind it was of him to bring you all the way to Monkswood on such a night.'

Realising she was expected to add something, Loris agreed woodenly, 'Yes, wasn't it?'

Isobel turned to Jonathan and, as though to make up for her daughter's marked lack of sociability, said, 'I'm so pleased Loris managed to persuade you to stay.' Then, without much hope, 'Do you play whist or bridge by any chance?'

'Both. Though not particularly well.'

'At the last minute Colonel Jefferson couldn't come, so anyone who plays cards at all will be a welcome addition to our little party.'

'Oh, but Mr Drummond can't possibly stay for the rest of the weekend,' Loris said with more force than politeness.

Looking surprised by her daughter's vehemence, Isobel pointed out, 'It would make sense. Apparently the Elder has overflowed its banks and quite a few of the local roads are flooded, so the journey back to town could be very difficult.'

'But h-he wasn't prepared to stay.' Loris tried to sound practical rather than panic-stricken. 'I mean, it's a question of clothes and things…'

'Clothes aren't a problem. Luckily Jonathan and Simon are much of a size, and Simon has a whole wardrobe of things he hasn't even worn.'

With a speaking glance at him, Loris said, 'But I'm sure Mr Drummond—'

Face straight, but a wicked gleam in his eyes, he broke in, 'Oh, surely we know each other well enough for you to call me Jonathan.'

Biting her lip, she went on, 'I'm sure *Jonathan* has to get back. We can't expect him to—'

'As I've already told your mother, I'd be delighted to stay,' he broke in smoothly.

Wondering what he was up to, Loris glared at him in helpless fury.

'There! You see, it's all settled,' Isobel said a little testily, 'and has been for the past half-hour. I'm having Simon's bed made up for Jonathan so that if Mark manages to get here after all he can have his usual room. Though he seemed doubtful at first—'

'You've spoken to him?'

'He rang up about twenty minutes ago to apologise for his absence and say he was sorry not to have come down as planned.'

'Does Dad know?'

Isobel shook her head. 'Your father went straight out

after breakfast. He's with Reynolds, checking on reported storm damage to some of the cottages on the estate.'

'When you talked to Mark, did he tell you what had happened last night?' Loris asked cautiously.

'Apparently Alan Gresham's daughter suddenly felt unwell, and because no taxi was immediately available, he offered to drive her home...'

Catching Jonathan's eye, Loris saw a kind of amused contempt there.

'As your father and I had already left, it's just as well that Mark was on hand to do duty as a host.'

Judging by Isobel's insouciance, she hadn't the faintest idea that Alan Gresham's daughter and 'that blonde creature' were one and the same.

'He said he'd get hold of you and, if conditions allowed, possibly bring you down in time for lunch. He seemed very surprised when I told him you were already here...'

I bet he did, Loris thought cynically.

'The whole thing, it seems, was a misunderstanding. He couldn't find you to tell you what was happening, and then when he got back to the hotel you were nowhere to be seen and almost everyone had gone. He thought that, because of the weather, you must have made up your mind to go straight home instead of coming down here.'

Obviously wondering if they'd had a quarrel, her mother asked, 'What made you decide to come without him?'

'My flat was occupied.'

'Occupied?'

'I've lent it to Judy and Paul for last night and tonight.'

'Even so—'

'They're on their honeymoon.'

'Oh. Still, it's worked out quite well. Or rather will have done when Mark gets here.'

'I thought you said he might not be coming?'

'He seemed doubtful at first, but as soon as he knew you

were here he said he was definitely going to try to get down.'

Loris found herself hoping fervently that he wouldn't succeed. The situation would be quite bad enough when her father discovered what had happened, without Mark's presence adding to the problems.

'Though I don't know what his chances are...'

'If he stays on the main road as far as Harefield, and then takes Dewy Lane, which runs along higher ground, he might manage to get through,' Jonathan said with a cheerful optimism that grated on Loris's frayed nerves.

Vexedly, she wondered why he sounded so laid-back, so unconcerned at the prospect of the other man arriving?

Probably he imagined she would keep quiet about what had happened the previous night. And if things had been different, unwilling to broadcast her shame, she no doubt would have done. But what he didn't know, so had failed to take into account, was the unfortunate meeting with her father.

Once Mark and her father had talked, the fat would be in the fire. As well as being furious with *her*, both men would be out for Jonathan's blood, and there was bound to be trouble.

Plainly surprised, Isobel was saying, 'It sounds as if you know this part of the world well?'

'I do.'

'Then you haven't always lived in the States?'

'Only for the past few years. I was born and brought up quite near here.'

'Oh!' She beamed at him. 'Then possibly you know Sir Hugh Drummond?'

Loris sighed. Her mother, who was from a relatively modest background and always tried to hide it, was a downright snob.

Jonathan raised a fair brow. 'The rich and aristocratic owner of Merriton Hall?'

Oblivious to the irony, she said, 'Yes. Is he any relation—your father, perhaps?'

Watching his hostess's face, he told her calmly, 'My father was a poor GP.'

Looking on, Loris wondered why he'd deliberately added 'poor'. Had he got a chip on his shoulder about not being well off? Or was he making a point of some kind?

Hurriedly changing the subject, Isobel said with forced brightness, 'I'm afraid we've made no real plans for today. Outdoor sporting activities seem to be largely ruled out. Mark, who used to play rugby for his school, was intending to fill in as a forward for the local team, but the game's been cancelled because the pitch is under water. However, we have a squash court and a games room, and there's a billiard table in the library. There's also a late-morning service at St Barnabas that I and some of our guests are planning to go to, if you'd care to join us?'

'Thank you. But I thought I might persuade Loris into taking a walk with me.' Addressing Loris, he went on, 'It isn't raining, and it shouldn't be too bad underfoot if we walk up to and along Stonywood Ridge.'

She needed a walk, but the last thing she wanted was Jonathan Drummond's company.

About to politely refuse, she thought better of it. His continuing presence at Monkswood was only going to invite more trouble, but if she could get him to where they wouldn't be overheard and warn him he might see sense and decide to leave as soon as possible.

'A walk sounds like a good idea,' she said with what cordiality she could muster. 'I could do with a breath of fresh air and some exercise.'

Looking somewhat surprised by her daughter's prompt acceptance, Isobel said, 'In that case I'll go and get ready for church. See you at lunchtime. With a bit of luck Mark will be here by then.'

An unholy gleam in his eye, Jonathan murmured, 'That sounds like fun.'

Ignoring his remark, Loris jumped to her feet. Just in case her father returned, the sooner they were out of the house the better she'd like it. 'Well, if you want to go for that walk…'

'Indeed I do.' Following her from the now empty break-fast-room, he added, 'Though as evening shoes aren't ex-actly suitable for cross-country hikes, I may need to borrow a pair of brogues.'

'I take it you know which is Simon's room?' she asked curtly, leading the way upstairs.

'Yes. Isobel, as she insisted I call her, took me along there earlier.'

Watching his companion's soft mouth tighten, he smiled grimly. 'I'm quite aware that you would sooner I'd just sneaked off like some criminal, or even vanished in a puff of smoke, rather than meet your mother.' As Loris's colour rose, he added, 'But when I was on my way downstairs, I ran into her…'

It seemed to be the morning for unfortunate meetings, Loris thought with wry humour.

'I was forced to explain my presence, and why I was still wearing evening dress. She was very gracious.'

'Yes, she would be,' Loris said drily, remembering his impeccable evening clothes.

Picking up her meaning instantly, he asked ironically, 'So you think it would have been better if I'd claimed kin-ship with Sir Hugh Drummond?'

'No, I don't. And if you're expecting me to apologise for her snobbery…'

'I'm not. You can hardly be held responsijble for her faults. Though she may well be responsible for yours.'

Loris flinched. 'If you think I wanted you to go because I was ashamed of you—'

'Didn't you?'

Golden eyes flashing, she denied, 'No, I most certainly did not. I *was* ashamed. But it was of myself.'

He gave her a keen, curious glance. 'I don't—'

They had reached the door of her room and, before he could complete whatever it was he was going to say, she turned the knob and asked quickly, 'Perhaps we can get ready and talk later?'

'By all means.' Without further ado, he disappeared in the direction of Simon's room.

As soon as Loris had replaced her thin waistcoat with a cream wool jumper, and changed into walking shoes and an anorak, she hurried back.

He was waiting in the corridor, similarly attired.

They left the house without speaking and, following the old red brick wall that bounded the Monkswood Estate, took the path that ran between it and the woods.

It was cold with a blustery wind but, though the clouds looked threatening, the impending rain had held off. They were both bare-headed, and collars turned up around their ears, they walked briskly, avoiding a litter of small branches and storm debris.

When they reached clearer, rising ground, she slowed a little and, walking side by side, they fell comfortably into step. He seemed appreciably taller this morning, and she realised it was because she was wearing flat heels.

She was wondering how to broach the subject of his leaving when he broke the silence to say, 'After your initial rather *cool* reception, I'm curious to know why you agreed to come walking with me.' Mockingly he added, 'I don't suppose it was because you wanted my company?'

'You don't suppose right,' she informed him shortly. 'I wanted to ask you to go.'

'Tell me something. Is it just *me* you can't bear the sight of? Or do you prefer all your one-night stands to quietly disappear the following morning?'

'How dare you?' she choked, almost too furious to speak. 'I don't go in for one-night stands. Last night was the first and only time I've ever...'

'Cheated on your fiancé?' he suggested, as she paused to search for the right words.

'Allowed myself to be seduced.'

'Without wishing to sound ungallant, may I point out that you *invited* it.'

'I did no such thing,' she flared.

'You came back to my room on the pretext of bringing me a razor—'

'That *wasn't* a pretext.' Seeing he was far from convinced, she insisted, '*Truly* it wasn't.'

He frowned. 'Why don't you admit that the whole thing was just another game of tit-for-tat?'

'Tit-for-tat?' she echoed blankly.

'Your fiancé had gone off with another woman, so you invited me to stay the night, to have his room, so that I was *handy*, so to speak.'

Remembering the little scene on the dance floor, she stopped walking abruptly and turned to him, a look of horror on her face. 'You don't honestly think that? Think I was just *using* you to retaliate?'

'What else can I think?'

Suddenly it seemed very important to convince him that she'd had no such intention. 'You're wrong. Quite wrong,' she cried passionately. 'I may have a lot of faults, but I'm not that kind of woman. A kiss on a dance floor, when everyone else was kissing, would have been one thing, but I would never have dreamt of going to those lengths...'

'Well, if it wasn't a spot of retaliation, and you don't go

in for one-night stands, why did you come back to my room?'

'I've told you.'

'You mean it really *was* just to bring me a razor?'

'Yes.'

'Then all I can say is you're remarkably naïve.'

'Stupid would be a better word,' she corrected him bitterly.

He took both her hands in his and said gently, 'I'm sorry.'

'For thinking so badly of me? Or for seducing me?'

'Both. I'm not in the habit of seducing other men's fiancées, except...'

'Except when they invite it?'

Shaking his head, he said, 'I'm sorry, I completely misread the signs. I thought you wanted me to make love to you as much as I wanted to. It seemed a—' He broke off abruptly, then went on, 'I should have realised I was mistaken when you ran like a frightened rabbit this morning. Believe me, I didn't mean it to be like this, and I blame myself very much.' He released her hands. 'If you'd like to go back to the house now, I'll leave as soon as I've changed.'

It was what she had wanted to hear, yet, fundamentally honest, she found she couldn't let him go thinking he was entirely to blame.

Lifting her chin, her face as red as a poppy, she said, 'It's quite true that the razor wasn't a pretext; it's also true that I've never before indulged in casual sex—'

He raised an eyebrow at the *casual*. 'I thought it was rather more than that.'

'How could it be? Two virtual strangers...'

'Did the fact that we were virtual strangers matter? Wasn't how we made each other feel much more important?'

When, not knowing quite what to say, she remained silent, he pursued, 'I thought you enjoyed it as much as I did. Was I wrong again?'

No, he wasn't wrong. It had been wonderful, but she wasn't about to tell him so.

Ignoring the question, she went on doggedly, 'The point I'm making is that you weren't wholly to blame. I'm as responsible for what happened as you are. I *did* want you to make love to me.'

With betraying candour, she added, 'It's so *unlike* me. That's why I couldn't face you this morning. I felt dreadfully ashamed. I thought you'd think I was *easy*. In the event, you thought even worse of me.'

'For which I'm sincerely sorry.'

'I'm sorry too. Sorry for involving you in something that could have very unpleasant consequences.'

He gazed down at her enchanting face. Her golden eyes were serious beneath a black, wind-ruffled fringe, her small nose was red with cold and her generous mouth looked pinched.

Suppressing a powerful desire to kiss some colour into those pale lips, he said abruptly, 'Let's walk on. It's getting cold standing here.'

Because her mind was on other things, Loris had scarcely noticed the cold until then. But as he spoke she became aware that her feet were numb and her whole body was chilled and on the verge of shivering. Trying to stop her teeth chattering, she objected, 'But I thought we were going back.'

'It's a fair way back, and you look half-frozen. What if we walk as far as the Lamb and Flag—it'll only take a couple of minutes—and have a pot of hot coffee?'

She was torn. The prospect of some hot coffee was a very welcome one, but at the same time she wanted him safely out of the way before Mark arrived and her father discovered what had happened.

As she hesitated, Jonathan took her hand. 'Come on, it's starting to rain.' Fingers twined in hers, he began to hurry her up the lane that led to the pub.

The Lamb and Flag, a picturesque black and white half-timbered building with overhanging eaves and a decided list to starboard, was an old coaching inn, left mercifully unmodernised.

Inside, the white walls were of rough plaster, and the low ceiling was oak-beamed. In the inglenook fireplace at the far end of the room a huge log fire blazed and crackled. The floor was made of grey stone slabs, polished smooth by time and the passage of many feet.

At the moment, however, the place was empty, apart from the buxom landlady behind the bar who was replacing glasses.

'Nasty cold morning,' she greeted them cheerfully.

'It is,' Jonathan agreed.

As though to add point to their words, a flurry of sleet was thrown against the leaded windows.

'What will you have?' She gave them a big, hospitable smile.

'Can you manage a large pot of coffee?'

'I can indeed. If you want to take a seat by the fire, I'll fetch it over to you.'

Having helped Loris off with her anorak, Jonathan removed his own and hung them both on one of the large wooden pegs just inside the door.

She saw that he'd replaced his jacket with a dark-green sweater that made him look even fairer, and even more attractive.

Feeling the unwelcome pull of that attraction, she carefully avoided his eyes as they crossed to the fire. When they were comfortably ensconced in front of it, Loris took off her shoes and stretched her icy feet gratefully to the warmth. Some life was returning to them by the time the landlady brought over the coffee and two heated pottery mugs.

Addressing them both, she said, 'Though we're not expecting many customers on a morning like this, there'll be some food ready in about half an hour, if you want to eat.' Then, to Jonathan, 'It's one of your favourites today. Chicken and pasta bake.'

'It sounds as if you're a regular,' Loris remarked as the landlady disappeared kitchenwards.

'I've popped in a few times since I've been back,' he said casually.

'I thought you lived in town?'

'Yes, I do, during the week. But since I returned to England I've been in this area most weekends, visiting old haunts.'

Loris reached to pour the coffee, which was good and hot and accompanied by thick, country cream and brown sugar.

She didn't usually take either, but, with no weight problem to worry about, she treated herself to a spoonful of sugar and a generous helping of cream, while Jonathan drank his black.

Both their cups had been drained and replenished, and Loris was trying to think of the best way to tell him what he would have to know, when he pre-empted her by remarking, 'You mentioned something about unpleasant consequences…'

'Yes.' She sighed. 'When Mark finds out what's happened, he's bound to be livid.'

'I wouldn't have thought he had any justification for being livid,' Jonathan remarked levelly. 'After all, he was, in a manner of speaking, the first to stray from the fold.'

'He's not likely to take that into account. In any case,

two wrongs don't make a right—' even as she spoke, Loris was unhappily aware how very prim and self-righteous she sounded '—and in a way, I drove him to it.'

Jonathan's fair, well-marked brows rose. '*You* drove him to it? Surely you don't mean by being late for the party?'

'Well, partly… Though there was a lot more to it than that.'

'A growing incompatibility?' he hazarded.

'Certainly not.' Seeing he was waiting for an explanation, her colour rising, she added, 'It's something I'd rather not talk about.'

'But because you feel guilty, to salve your conscience, you intend to confess all?'

'No. The truth is, I don't have much option. You see, when I was leaving your room this morning I ran into my father in the corridor. I was carrying my clothes. Last night's party dress…'

'Ah! A dead giveaway.' Humorously, he added, 'So why didn't he come bursting in with a shotgun?'

'Because it was Mark's room, and he didn't realise that Mark hadn't come down as planned.'

'I see… And of course he was used to you sleeping with your fiancé?'

As she began to shake her head he said, 'No, that doesn't make sense. If your parents know you two sleep together, why were you given separate rooms? Surely it wasn't just for the look of the thing?'

'They don't know.'

'Then you were quite used to corridor creeping?'

'No,' she said sharply.

He lifted a quizzical brow. 'You mean if you were under your parents' roof you went all Victorian?'

She failed to answer, and he queried thoughtfully, 'When your father saw you leaving, as he thought, Longton's bed, was he unhappy about it?'

'The contrary, I think, after what had happened at the party. You see, Mark and he have always got along very well, and he's looking forward to having him for a son-in-law…'

'That's understandable. They're similar types.'

'No, not really…' But even as she started to deny it she knew he was right; they *were* similar types. Her mother had already spotted it.

Though she had done her utmost, Loris had never really got along with her father. Now, made uncomfortable by the sudden realisation of how alike he and her fiancé were, she bit her lip.

'So, while he had no objection to you sleeping with Longton, there'll almost certainly be the devil to pay when he discovers that it *wasn't* Longton you'd spent the night with.'

'Exactly,' she said. Adding with renewed urgency, 'That's why I want you to leave before Mark gets here and he *does* find out.'

'I'm not much for running. Unless you've decided to run with me?'

'No, I haven't. What would be the use? I'll have to face them all some time, so I may as well get it over with. But the sooner *you* go the better…'

She reached for her shoes in preparation for leaving.

A hand on her arm, he stopped her. 'There's no hurry. As it's already gone twelve…'

Gone twelve! She hadn't realised how late it was.

'…and I can vouch for the cooking, I suggest we grab a spot of lunch before we start back.'

As she began to shake her head, he asked coaxingly, 'Wouldn't you sooner lunch here, just the two of us in front of a good fire, rather than at Monkswood?'

The true answer was yes. Almost anything would be preferable to lunching at home. But there simply wasn't time.

'You didn't have any breakfast,' he went on, 'so you must be getting hungry.'

'No... No, I'm not.'

'Well, I am.'

Her agitation obvious, she insisted, 'But we haven't *time* to stay for lunch. Surely you can get something to eat on the way back to London?'

'I've decided not to go back just yet.'

'But you *must*...'

Mark was possessive, and tended to be jealous for no good reason. On one occasion he'd threatened to knock a waiter down merely for 'ogling' her.

Now there *was* a good reason she shuddered to think what might happen. If he lost his temper and it came to a fight Jonathan was a few inches shorter, slimly built and a good three stone lighter.

'Mark can be very intimidating when he loses his temper,' she added.

'Dear me,' Jonathan said mildly. 'I really can't think of anything worse than being intimidated by a six-feet-four-inch rugby forward.'

She gritted her teeth. 'I wish you'd be serious.'

'You think I'm not?'

'This is no laughing matter. He'll be absolutely furious.'

'Won't he be furious with you too?'

'Yes,' she admitted. 'But he wouldn't hit a woman—'

She broke off as the landlady emerged to say, 'If you want to eat, it's just ready. Shall I bring it through?'

Loris was about to politely refuse when Jonathan answered easily, 'That would be great, Mrs Lawson.'

As Mrs Lawson bustled away, Loris begged desperately. '*Please,* Jonathan...'

'It's nice of you to be so concerned about me.'

'It's not *nice*, it's *necessary*. You've never seen Mark

when he's in a rage. While he wouldn't dream of hitting a woman, he'll have no compunction about beating up a man.'

'And you faint at the sight of blood?'

Concerned for his safety, and angry with him for treating the whole thing so lightly, she felt her eyes fill with tears of frustration. 'Don't you see? If you get hurt I'll feel to blame.'

Taking her hand, he raised it to his lips and said gently, 'There's no need to worry. While I'm far from being Superman, I'm not exactly a seven-stone weakling. I can take care of myself.'

Suddenly, without rhyme or reason, she felt it likely that he could.

As though reading her mind, he smiled at her and suggested, 'So why don't you forget about it and enjoy your lunch?'

'I'm not sure I can,' she admitted, blinking away the tears.

'Afraid *I'll* beat *him* up?' he asked quizzically.

Smiling in spite of herself, she shook her head. Then said in a heartfelt voice, 'It's all such a *mess*.'

'Some good may come of it.'

'*No* good will come of it,' she corrected. 'Have you stopped to think that with both my father and Mark gunning for you, your job might well be on the line?'

'I must admit I hadn't.'

'That was why I was hoping you'd go before anyone had seen you or knew who you were. Now it's too late…' With a sudden flare of hope, she added, 'Unless I could persuade Mother to forget all about you.'

'I should imagine it's a bit late to try,' Jonathan said matter-of-factly. 'Both your mother and father will almost certainly be back home by now. And, unless he's encountered any major problems, Longton should be there too… Ah, here's lunch.'

CHAPTER FOUR

THOUGH convinced she couldn't eat a thing, at Jonathan's insistence Loris tried the chicken and pasta bake and found it very tasty.

'Keep eating,' he urged. 'Things may be in a mess, but starving yourself isn't going to help matters.'

Knowing he was right, she obeyed, and found she was hungry after all.

'Mmm, delicious,' she murmured as she finished the last bite. 'It's equally as nice as they make at Il Lupo.'

'Where and what is Il Lupo?'

'A little basement restaurant quite close to Piccadilly. If I'm eating in town and I'm anywhere near Shear Lane I usually have lunch there. The food's good and remarkably cheap.'

'With a rich father I wouldn't have thought *cheap* was a necessary factor.'

'What has having a rich father got to do with it? I've been independent since I left school.'

'Surely he helped you get through college?'

'No. I took weekend and evening jobs to do that.'

'Why should a wealthy man leave his only daughter to fend for herself?'

'Perhaps he thought it would be character-building. Or Mother might be right when she calls him an old skinflint.'

Afraid of Jonathan pursuing the matter, she was relieved when Mrs Lawson appeared with wedges of golden-crusted apple pie and stilton, and piled more logs onto the fire before going to serve a couple of men at the bar.

The two men had drunk their pints and left before she returned with a freshly made pot of coffee.

'An excellent meal,' Jonathan congratulated her. 'It's a pity more people weren't here to enjoy it.'

'Things are always quiet at this time of the year, but now there's only Arthur and me to run the place it suits me fine. Just ring the bell on the bar if you want any more coffee.'

As Loris started to pour the steaming liquid Jonathan's eyes fixed on the magnificent half-hoop of diamonds she wore, and he asked casually, 'How long have you been engaged?'

'Three months.'

'Any wedding plans?'

'Nothing's settled yet...' Mark had wanted an early-spring wedding, but, feeling panicky at the thought of being rushed, Loris had pleaded for a summer wedding. 'Though we've talked about getting married at the end of June.'

'You said Longton will be furious with you... Do you think he'll want to end the engagement?'

With quiet confidence, she answered, 'No, I'm sure he won't.'

'What about you? Do *you* want to end it?'

'I don't think so.'

She wanted a husband, a home and a family while she was still young, and Mark had been the first man to attract her since Nigel.

'In spite of how he treated you last night?'

'I've told you, it was very largely my own fault.'

'So, apart from being late, what did you do to upset him enough to make him want to take another woman to bed?'

She half shook her head, wishing he'd let the subject drop.

But, refusing to, he persisted, 'After seeing them together on the dance floor, you don't seriously believe he took Miss Gresham home because she was ill?'

'No, I don't.'

'And you're not angry about it?'

'Of course I'm angry. But, as I keep saying, I was partly to blame.'

'Tell me how?'

Seeing he had no intention of giving up, she said wearily, 'When I went over to Mark to apologise for being so late he started talking about how beautiful Pamela Gresham was and how she fancied him. He was hoping to make me jealous...'

'Any particular reason?' Jonathan queried.

'He wanted me to agree to sleep with him that night, but because we were going to be at Monkswood I refused. I didn't like the idea of sleeping with him under my parents' roof.'

Realising how ridiculous that must sound in the circumstances, she blushed hotly before going on, 'He tried to persuade me, but I still didn't feel comfortable about it. He wasn't in a mood to take no for an answer, and suggested that we went back to his flat before going down to Paddleham. I was about to agree, when he got impatient and said something like, "I'm warning you. This time, I don't intend to take no for an answer—"'

Suddenly realising how revealing those words were, she stopped in dismay.

Noting the *this time*, and adding it to what he already knew, Jonathan asked carefully, 'So what did you say?'

'I lost my temper and told him he'd have to. He said, "Damn it, if you won't come back to my flat with me, I know someone who will."'

'He meant Miss Gresham, of course?'

Loris nodded. 'He boasted, "She'd come like a shot, and I might just ask her." I said, "Why don't you?" and walked away.'

'Good for you!' Jonathan applauded.

'But, don't you see, if I *hadn't*, if I'd agreed to go back to his flat, none of this would have happened and we wouldn't be in this mess.'

'Did you *want* to go back to his flat?'

'Not really,' she admitted, looking down. 'After what had happened I wasn't in the right mood. But I thought it was time I...'

Narrowed eyes on her face, he probed, 'Time you *what*? Went to bed with him?'

He watched the sweep of dark lashes flicker against her high cheekbones before she said, 'Yes.'

'But you hadn't previously.' It was a statement rather than a question.

The fact that she had never slept with Mark was something she would have preferred Jonathan not to know. It raised too many questions. Yet she couldn't bring herself to lie about it.

When she failed to deny it, he pursued, 'Do you love him?'

'I do.' Then, almost as if she was trying to convince herself, 'Of course I do.'

'So why haven't you slept with him? It's almost the norm these days to go to bed with one's fiancé.'

Wanting to tell him to mind his own business, she found herself saying weakly, 'For several reasons. It's a long story.'

'I've got all day.'

At her instinctive rejection of that, he said, 'Now it's this late there's no point in rushing back, so tell me why you haven't slept with Longton. He must have kept pressing you to?'

Knowing that Jonathan wasn't about to drop the subject until she told him what he wanted to know, she gave in to the pressure. 'Yes, he did. But I...'

'Kept putting him off?'

'Yes.'

'I'm curious to know why. He's a good-looking, macho man, if you like that type—and you obviously do or you wouldn't be engaged to him—and you're a warm, passionate woman.'

'But I'm not really.'

'You were last night.' Watching her cheeks grow warm, and thinking how beautiful she was, he probed, 'What gave you the idea you weren't?'

Looking anywhere but at him, she admitted, 'I'd had a previous relationship that didn't work out. It left me feeling disillusioned and…inadequate.'

Without really knowing why, she found herself telling him about Nigel.

She had never even told Mark about Nigel. Perhaps because they seldom really *talked*. As well as watching a lot of sport on TV, Mark liked parties and entertaining, getting out and about. And on the few occasions they did have time for a conversation he tended to take it over. He was a talker rather than a listener.

Studying her expressive face, Jonathan asked, 'How old were you then?'

'Eighteen.'

His jaw tightened, as though he felt either anger or pain. 'And you say you were engaged? Did your father and mother approve?'

'Yes, they were all for it. Nigel's parents were family friends.'

'And doubtless rich?'

'Yes.'

'Was that why you agreed to marry him?'

'No, it wasn't. If you must know, I thought I was in love with him.'

'So what happened? Why did you finally break up?'

She told him why, flatly, dispassionately, adding, 'Somehow, being treated like that destroyed my confidence in myself as a woman...'

'But surely it was different next time?'

'There was no next time.'

'You mean you've steered clear of men all these years because that selfish young swine not only cheated on you but made you half believe you were frigid?'

'Not entirely.' She strove to be fair. 'No one had attracted me enough to make me *want* to try again, until I met Mark.'

'But you've just admitted that you've kept even *him* at arm's length.'

'Yes.' Looking into the flames, she sighed. 'I didn't really *intend* to. Somehow it just happened...'

The same as last night had just happened. But in the opposite way.

His eyes on her half-averted face, he remarked softly, 'Knowing you're anything but frigid, it strikes me as odd that you weren't willing to sleep with someone you've told me you love.'

Something about the way he spoke made her look at him. He was smiling a little, as though well satisfied.

Realising with a shock of surprise how she had bared her soul, as well as her body, to a man who was scarcely more than a stranger, she felt her throat go dry.

Swallowing hard, she waited for him to ask the obvious question. A question she had yet to find an answer to. *So why me?*

But with a sensitivity she could only be heartily thankful for, he smoothly changed the subject. 'You mentioned you were an interior designer... What does your work involve? Selecting furniture? Fabrics? Colour schemes?'

'Quite often the lot. And every project is a new challenge. That's what makes it so fascinating...'

All at once there was a feeling of ease, a rapport between them.

'It would have been fun to design for my own place,' she added wistfully, 'but all I could find to rent was a furnished flat. Though I suppose from a purely practical point of view that's given me more time for my clients.'

'How do you choose your clients?'

'I don't. They choose me. I follow up every enquiry, and make suggestions and preliminary sketches, but unfortunately I don't always get the job.'

'Can't you charge for wasted time?'

'Not until I'm better known. At the moment I have to offer the first consultation free, and as the rent they charge for my flat is exorbitant, when I fail to get a job I have to tighten my belt.'

'With a wealthy fiancé?'

'I wouldn't dream of asking Mark to help.'

Letting that go, he suggested, 'Some places must be harder to design for than others?'

'Some *clients* are harder to design for than others... They ask advice, but they already have a preconceived idea in their minds of what they actually want. Sometimes it takes some winkling out, and even when I've succeeded it isn't always easy to translate it into a workable scheme. But there's nothing I would rather do, and when something works, and you *know* it's right, there's a tremendous amount of job satisfaction...'

Temporarily forgetting all the troubles the weekend had brought, she became animated as, responding to his interest, she talked with fluency and enthusiasm about her love of colour and design, and her pleasure in her work.

'It sounds like a passion that will last a lifetime,' he observed.

Some of the sparkle died out of her face. 'Mark wants

me to stop working after we're married,' she said flatly. 'He said a rich man's wife has no need to work.'

'*Financial* need, no. But there are other considerations just as important.'

'Mark doesn't seem to think so.'

'So what will you do with yourself?'

'Apart from sit and count my money all day? I don't really know.'

It was a sore point, and, turning away, she began to pull on her shoes. 'It's time we were getting back.'

'Perhaps you're right.'

Strolling over to the bar, he rang the large brass bell that waited there and, when Mrs Lawson appeared, paid her for the meal, adding a generous tip.

'Will we see you next weekend?' she asked.

'I'm not sure. It all depends.'

'Well, all I can say is I hope it's better weather next time.'

When Loris had added her thanks to Jonathan's, they pulled on their anoraks and made their way outside into the greyness.

A mixture of rain and snow was being driven before a bleak, easterly wind, and after the comfortable warmth of the fire it felt bitter.

Heads down, and walking as quickly as possible, they set off back. Neither was wearing gloves, and Jonathan walked with his hands thrust deep into his pockets.

Loris did the same, but the pockets in her anorak, which was fashionable rather than practical, were too shallow to afford much protection.

Glancing sideways at her, Jonathan asked, 'All right?'

'Yes.'

He reached to take hold of her hand and, finding it was like ice, returned both his hand and hers to the warmth of his pocket.

There was something *caring* about the gesture that brought an odd little lump to her throat.

The rain grew heavier, and soon they were both soaked to the skin. In spite of all the problems that loomed ahead, when the house came into view it was a welcome sight, its lighted windows suggesting warmth and comfort.

Hoping against hope that they wouldn't meet anyone, Loris chose to go in by the rear door, and to use the back staircase.

They were lucky, and made it upstairs without seeing a soul. At her bedroom door, she turned to glance at the man by her side.

His neat ears were red and his thick lashes were beaded with moisture; his hair was plastered against his skull and rivulets of water ran down his face. But, despite his saturated state, he had an air of ease, of calm self-assurance.

'No one's seen us come back,' she said with relief, 'so if you get changed as quickly as possible—'

'I was looking forward to a hot, leisurely shower,' he said plaintively.

'But don't you see? There's still a chance...'

'To do what?'

'To *leave*, of course.' Urgently, she added, 'Go out the way we came in, and when you've got your car turn left and take the back drive—'

'And leave you to face the music alone?'

'It's what I *want* you to do. Facing them won't be pleasant, but no one will do *me* any harm.' She put a hand on his arm and shook him. 'Go, while there's still a chance. Staying will only add to the problems.'

'That's a matter of opinion.'

'It's a matter of *fact*,' she hissed at him. 'Your presence is bound to inflame Mark... Oh, *please*, Jonathan, go.'

'We're in this together, and the only way I'll go is if you go with me.'

Though she was tempted, she shook her head. 'What would be the good of that?'

'Exactly. There's no point in either of us running away. The best thing by far would be to have a showdown and get it over with.'

He sounded almost as if he was enjoying the prospect.

Opening the door to her room, he gently pushed her inside. 'Now, why don't you go and get out of those wet things before you catch a chill?'

Accepting that she wasn't going to budge him, she went through to the bathroom and stripped off.

Standing under the steaming water, she waited until her frozen body was thawed out before reaching for the shampoo.

As well as the comfort the hot water brought, she felt an inner glow of warmth. Though common sense insisted that it would have been better if Jonathan had gone, she felt a sneaking relief that he had refused to leave her to face things alone.

When she had towelled herself thoroughly, and rubbed her hair, she put on a fleecy robe and went to find some dry clothes.

Dressed in a grey skirt and a fine woollen blouse the colour of wet lilac, she brushed her hair and made-up lightly. Then, mentally girding her loins, she went out, closing the door behind her.

Jonathan was strolling down the corridor towards her. His hair had dried to what she now recognised as its normal corn-colour, and was smoothly brushed. He was wearing well-cut trousers and a black polo-necked sweater that made him look both attractive and oddly dangerous.

Wondering what had made a word like *dangerous* spring to mind, she realised it was something to do with his quiet, but absolute, confidence.

Hands loose by his sides, a glint in his eyes, he was

whistling something half under his breath. It was, she recognised after a moment, the theme from *High Noon*.

'That sense of humour will get you into trouble one day,' she said crossly.

He grinned, white teeth gleaming. 'Ah, so you like old movies?'

Responding to his charm, she admitted, 'Better than some of the modern ones.'

'Remember *The Ghost and Mrs Muir*...?'

'Oh, yes... And *The Babysitter*...'

Discussing their favourite black and white films, they made their way downstairs.

They were crossing the spacious hall when the library door opened and Mark came out. His tense expression changed to one of mingled annoyance and relief when he saw Loris.

'Where on earth have you been? Your mother said you'd gone out for a walk mid-morning.'

'Yes, that's right.' She was surprised by how steady her voice sounded.

'You've been out so long I was beginning to think you'd gone back to town instead.'

'We stopped for coffee,' Jonathan said smoothly, 'and when it came on to rain I persuaded Loris to stay at the pub for lunch.'

Mark's heavy head swung round, and he glared at the younger man. 'What the hell are you up to, Drummond?'

At that moment Mrs Delacost came down the stairs and crossed the hall, holding a package in her hand.

Glancing curiously at the little group, she addressed Loris, 'I wonder if you happen to know where Sir Peter is? I've some pictures taken in Monte I promised to show him.'

'I'm afraid I don't—'

'I've just this minute been speaking to him.' Mark produced a charming smile. 'He rang to apologise for leaving his guests so long, but unfortunately he's been delayed by a slight accident.'

'Oh, dear! He wasn't hurt, I hope?'

'No, I'm happy to say. He and his bailiff were returning from checking on storm damage to the estate when a plank bridge they were driving over collapsed and the Land Rover ended up in the stream.

'Luckily the water was only a few feet deep, so neither man was in any real danger. At the moment they're trying to drag the Land Rover out with a tractor.'

'Oh, dear, I'm so sorry. So terribly sorry. Poor, poor Sir Peter! What a perfectly *dreadful* thing to happen, and just when—'

Mark cut short the commiserations. 'As our hostess is lying down with a migraine, I wonder if you'd be kind enough to tell the other guests what's happened and convey Sir Peter's sincere apologies?'

'Oh, certainly.' Apparently well pleased at being given such an important task, she hurried towards the sitting-room.

Seeing Mark was about to return to the attack, Loris suggested urgently, 'If there's no one in the library, let's go in there. We don't really want to stand about in the hall.'

The library was a big, handsome room, with a billiard table at one end and a low leather suite grouped around a glowing log fire. Twin standard lamps were burning and it was comfortably warm.

As soon as the door had closed behind them, and swinging to face the younger man, Mark said brusquely, 'I asked you what the hell you're up to.'

'Up to?' Jonathan drawled. 'I'm afraid I don't quite understand.'

'Don't come the innocent with me. First you push your nose in and ask Loris to dance, and then you go out of your way to drive her down here.'

'Well, if you remember, *you* were otherwise engaged.'

'What the devil do you know about it?'

Loris noticed that though Mark loomed over the other man somehow he failed to diminish him in the slightest. Size, she realised, wasn't important. Jonathan exuded a kind of quiet strength, a feeling of authority, that made him any man's equal.

Now he answered blandly, 'I happened to notice you leaving the hotel with another woman.'

'That's none of your damn business.'

'I decided to make it my business when I saw your fiancée standing abandoned in the rain.'

'So you turned into Sir Galahad?' Mark sneered.

'If I remember rightly, Galahad was a knight of immaculate purity, so I'm afraid the comparison is hardly fitting in view of—'

Terrified of what he was going to say next, Loris rushed into speech. 'Jonathan offered to drive me home when there were no taxis immediately available.'

'A likely story.'

Coldly, Loris remarked, 'I understood you drove *Pamela* home for the same reason?'

Looking momentarily disconcerted, Mark decided to ignore that and press on. 'But instead of taking you home Drummond drove you all the way down to Monkswood, no doubt hoping to get a foot in the door.'

'I couldn't go home because I'd lent my flat to Judy and her husband for the weekend, so I *asked* Jonathan to bring me here.'

'Well, it seems he made the most of the opportunity.'

'Driving conditions were so bad I begged him to stay the night.'

Mark grunted his displeasure. 'Well, it's now late afternoon, so what's he still doing here?'

Hating the way they were talking about Jonathan as

though he wasn't there, she said, 'Mother invited him to stay for the rest of the weekend.'

'If he wasn't *planning* on staying, how come he had clothes with him?'

'He didn't—'

'Isobel was kind enough to lend me some of her stepson's,' Jonathan finished evenly.

Loris felt sure he'd deliberately used her mother's name to rattle the older man.

If so, he'd succeeded.

Red in the face, Mark bit out, 'You're a damn sight too presumptuous. Who the hell gave you permission to call her Isobel?'

'She did.'

'No doubt because she thought you were *somebody*. How many lies did you tell her?'

'None.' A gleam in his eye, Jonathan admitted, 'Though I may have misled her a little.'

'I bet you did. Well, get it into your head that you don't belong here. You're not in our class, and never will be.'

'I think I can stand it.'

'Damn and blast your arrogance! Take it from me, Drummond, you've outstayed your welcome. You can leave as soon as you like.'

'I'll be happy to leave when *my hostess* tells me I'm no longer welcome.'

His brown eyes blazing with temper, Mark said, 'I've had more than enough of your insolence. You can get out of here now! This minute!'

Standing his ground, refusing to be intimidated, Jonathan murmured, 'Strange... I must have missed something somewhere. You see, I hadn't realised this was *your* house.'

Baring his teeth, Mark cried furiously, 'You think you're mighty clever, but if you don't leave of your own accord I'll have you thrown out.'

'Then you don't think you're big enough to do it personally?'

'Plenty big enough, and believe me it'll give me the greatest pleasure.'

'Don't!' Loris cried as Mark advanced threateningly on the younger man. 'This *isn't* your house and you've no right to throw anyone out of it.'

'*Try* to throw anyone out of it,' Jonathan goaded.

'You're asking for it,' Mark snarled.

'Leave it, Mark,' Loris said sharply. 'You know as well as I do that my father won't want any trouble when there's a house party going on.'

'So you feel you need to protect your Sir Galahad?' Mark sneered. 'Well, I bet he'll be only too happy to hide behind a woman's skirts... Won't you, Drummond?'

'Not at all. I'm quite capable of fighting my own battles.'

'Then why aren't you squaring up to me now?'

'Firstly because you're six inches taller and several stone heavier than I am. Secondly because I'm in someone else's home. And, thirdly, because I don't want to have to hurt you.'

Infuriated beyond endurance, Mark made a lunge at his tormentor.

Jonathan sidestepped and, using his opponent's weight and impetus to his own advantage, executed a textbook judo throw.

Mark's heavy body thudded onto the carpet and, half-winded, he lay for a second or two before struggling unsteadily to his feet. Shaking his head as if to clear it, he muttered, 'Why, you...!'

As he drew back his fist Loris cried, 'Stop it, the pair of you! How can you behave like this when at any moment one of the guests might walk in?'

Still groggy, Mark staggered a little, and, seizing his arm, she steered him to the nearest chair and pushed him into it.

Then, her knees feeling like jelly, she sat down abruptly in the chair opposite and glared angrily at Jonathan who, looking cool as a cucumber, was lounging against the mantel.

He raised his hands in mock surrender. 'I'm sorry.'

'So you should be. You're equally to blame.'

'You mean I should have let him throw me out?'

'I don't mean anything of the kind. But you know quite well you deliberately provoked him.'

'And you would have preferred me to have kowtowed?'

'No, I wouldn't. But I would have preferred you to have been a little more...' She hesitated, trying to find the right word.

'Conciliatory?' he suggested.

'Reasonable.'

'Do you really believe that my being "a little more reasonable" would have made any difference?'

Sighing inwardly, she silently admitted that she didn't. Mark had been out for blood from the word go. If Jonathan hadn't stood up to him he would only have taken it as a sign of weakness. Now at least, Mark being Mark, he would respect his adversary...

But it seemed she didn't know him after all.

'Damn you, Drummond,' Mark muttered. 'You may think you've won, but you're nothing short of a fool if you imagine I'm going to let someone like you get the better of me. *I'm* running BLC, and you're just a jumped-up office boy...'

'Oh, I'm a little more than that,' Jonathan said mildly.

'Well, whatever you are, you won't be with the firm much longer.'

'If that's a threat—'

Mark showed his teeth in a smile that was more like a

snarl. 'It is indeed. Make no mistake about it. You're for the chop.'

Loris's stomach tied itself in knots. Mark had reacted just as she'd first feared... And before he'd even discovered the worst.

But, appearing far from concerned, Jonathan was advising him coolly, 'As *Cosby's* own BLC, I doubt if you'll be able to get rid of me without their say-so.'

'I'll get their agreement, no matter what it takes.'

'Personal likes and dislikes don't figure in the equation. You'll have to put forward a good reason for dismissing me.'

'Don't worry, I'll find one. And if I can't find one I'll invent one.'

'I noticed you were pretty good at inventing things when Isobel gave us your version of why you drove Pamela Gresham home.'

Seeing Mark was about to explode, Loris took a deep breath and seized the initiative. She leaned forward and asked shortly, 'Do you still want to marry me?'

Startled, he said, 'What?'

Focusing all her attention, blotting out the man who was standing quietly in the background and forcing Mark to do the same, she repeated, 'I asked if you still want to marry me?'

'Of course I still want to marry you. You know I'm mad about you.'

'In view of what's happened I thought you might have changed your mind.'

'If you mean Pamela, before you start accusing me of anything, I told your mother—'

'She might believe that absurd story about taking the woman home because she was ill, but in view of what you said earlier I certainly don't.'

He ran a restless hand over his dark crinkly hair. 'Now

look here, Loris, I only said what I did to make you jealous. You must know I had no intention of going through with it.'

Ignoring his bluster, Loris demanded, 'Did you take her back to your flat?'

'No. Like I said, I took her to her place.'

'And you stayed.'

'No, no I didn't…' He couldn't look her in the eye.

'Come off it,' she said bluntly.

'Well, just for a coffee.'

'Don't take me for a fool, Mark.'

His face sullen, he said, 'All right, so I did stay. But it's your fault. You drove me to it. A man has needs.'

Guiltily, Loris had to acknowledge this as the truth. It had been partly her fault that Mark had gone off with Pamela, but she needed to make sure it never happened again.

'What about a woman?'

Looking nonplussed, he began, 'But you—'

'I'm talking in wider terms. If *men* have needs, wouldn't you agree that *women* do too?'

'Yes, I suppose so,' he said grudgingly.

'Only *suppose*?'

'Very well, they do. But it's different for a man.'

'In what way?'

'A man can satisfy those needs and it doesn't have to mean anything.'

'But not a woman?'

'With women it isn't just physical. They have to have emotional ties.'

'Is Pamela in love with you?'

'What? No, of course she isn't.'

'She merely fancied you?'

'Look, Loris—'

'So it *can* be purely physical?'

'All right, so it can.'

'And if a man can make love to a woman without it "meaning anything", and expect to be forgiven, then you must admit that the reverse is true?'

'Okay, I admit it.' Then, warily, 'Though I don't understand what you're getting at.'

'I'm trying to put paid to the old double standard that some men still cling to.'

'Men tend to be possessive about their women. It's natural.'

'But is it *just*? These days we have equality, so shouldn't it work both ways? You slept with Pamela and you expect me to forgive you, to go on as if nothing had changed...'

'Well, it hasn't—'

Cutting through his words, she demanded, 'But would you forgive me if I told you I'd slept with Jonathan last night?'

Knowing her too well to be alarmed, he asked with mock seriousness, 'Did you?'

'Yes,' she said baldly.

CHAPTER FIVE

JUST for an instant he looked shaken, then, obviously deciding it was merely an attempt to pay him back, he changed his expression to one of amused indulgence.

'I'm quite serious, Mark.'

Though his slight smile disappeared, she knew he didn't believe her.

He couldn't credit that she'd held him off for so long and then chosen to go to bed with a man she'd only just met. A man he'd contemptuously called a wimp and whom he still regarded as his social inferior.

But, pretending to take it seriously, he asked, 'So because you thought I was sleeping with someone else, you made up your mind to do the same?'

'I didn't make up my mind to do anything. It just happened. He was using your room...I took him one of Simon's razors...'

'Then I suppose he made a pass at you and you just couldn't resist his manly charms?'

Ignoring the sarcasm, she agreed quietly, 'Something like that.'

'Very well,' Mark said magnanimously, 'I forgive you. It's over and forgotten. We'll never mention it again.'

He totally refused to see the truth, she realised, because it was wounding to his pride, his self-esteem, to even *consider* that she might seriously have preferred another man to him.

'And you still want to marry me?'

'Yes, I still want to marry you. But I think it would make sense to bring the date forward. It's not as if we're planning on a big wedding, so instead of waiting until June let's get married as soon as possible.'

After a moment's thought, she said, 'I'll agree to that on two conditions.'

'What are they?'

'First, I'd like to keep on working...' Seeing his face darken, she specified, 'At least up until the time we *were* going to be married.'

'All right,' he agreed reluctantly. 'What's the second condition?'

This was the most important one, and Loris paused to choose her words with care. 'I want you to promise me that, no matter what, you won't take any further action against Jonathan.'

As though just remembering the other man's presence, Mark scowled in his direction.

'You seem mighty keen to protect him.'

'Please, Mark.'

'Very well, but I want *your* promise that you won't see him again, or have anything else to do with him.'

'I'll promise, in exchange for your assurance that you won't have anything else to do with Pamela—or any other woman for that matter.'

He nodded, and had the grace to flush slightly. 'I give you my word that I won't.' He smiled tentatively at her and Loris smiled back, convinced he meant it.

Then, turning to the younger man, who was still leaning against the mantel, his face inscrutable, Mark said curtly, 'And in the future you'd better keep your nose clean and stay well out of my way. In fact it would be no bad thing if you asked to be transferred back to the States...'

When his adversary said nothing, Mark added, his ego fully restored, 'Now, suppose you get out of here?'

Coolly, Jonathan informed him, 'I'll go when Loris asks me to.'

Just as he finished speaking the library door opened and Peter Bergman walked in. He was wearing smart country tweeds, and his iron-grey hair was smoothly brushed and still damp from the shower.

'What a day! The weather's absolutely foul, and I've been out since just after breakfast.' Then, to Mark, 'It's a pity you weren't with me. Reynolds isn't the most useful man in a crisis, and I could have done with your help.'

'I'm sorry I wasn't here in time.'

Peter frowned. 'But I thought... You didn't come down last night?'

'No, I was held up. I only got down here a couple of hours ago.'

His cold-blue eyes fixed on his daughter, Peter demanded, 'Then how did you get here?'

Before she could answer, Jonathan said levelly, 'I drove Loris down.'

As though becoming aware of the other man for the first time, Peter said, 'I know your face. You're with Cosby's aren't you? PA to William Grant?'

'That's right.'

'I'm afraid I can't recall your name.'

'Drummond. Jonathan Drummond.'

In answer to her father's unspoken *What the devil is he still doing here?* Loris explained, 'The conditions were so bad that I asked Jonathan to stay the night.'

'Which room did you put him in?'

It could have been a casual enquiry, but Loris knew only too well that it wasn't. Having gained assurance from her earlier stand, however, she replied steadily, 'Mark's.'

His face darkening with anger, Peter turned to glower at Jonathan.

Bearing in mind that there were now two people who had it in for him, and fearing the promise she'd extracted from Mark might not be enough to keep him out of trouble,

she added hurriedly, 'Mother did ask Jonathan to stay for
the rest of the weekend, but unfortunately he can't.'

She got to her feet and, turning to Jonathan, said for-
mally, 'Thank you for bringing me down. Now, I know
you want to be on your way before it gets too dark—' a
grey, murky dusk was already pressing against the windowpanes '—so have a good journey back.'

'You weren't thinking of coming with me?'

'No.' Swallowing, she held out her hand.

Taking it in his, he asked carefully, 'Quite sure you've
made the right decision?'

Knowing he was asking about a great deal more than
just going with him, she met his brilliant eyes without
flinching and said, 'Quite sure.'

'Then please give your mother my thanks and my apologies for leaving without seeing her.'

Becoming aware that he was still holding her hand, she
withdrew it abruptly. 'Goodbye.'

'Au revoir.'

Glancing from one man to the other, he sketched an
ironic salute, and a moment later the latch clicked quietly
behind him.

Staring at the closed door, knowing she would never see
him again, she felt a sudden surge of regret, a feeling of
loss and loneliness that was almost like a physical pain.

But she couldn't let herself feel like this about a virtual
stranger, a man she knew scarcely anything about.

She had opted to stay with Mark, to live the future she
had chosen, and so long as her father didn't wreck things
she would consider herself lucky.

Taking a deep breath, she turned to face her father.

He was standing with his back to the fire, looking like
an enraged turkeycock. His jowls quivering, he said, 'It
strikes me that for a man in his position Drummond's a
damn sight too sure of himself...'

Loris glanced uneasily at Mark, waiting for him to add *his* condemnation. She was surprised when he said nothing, until she realised that he would hardly want to lose face by mentioning his own humiliation.

'I don't know what the devil Isobel was thinking of, asking someone like him to stay.'

When no one made any comment, Peter demanded of his daughter, 'How long have you known him?'

'I met him for the first time last night.'

It wasn't at all the answer he'd been expecting, and he failed to hide his surprise.

'At the party?'

'Yes.'

'Did you know he was just an employee?'

'Yes, Mark told me.'

Well aware of how her father's mind worked, Loris guessed he was already starting to doubt the conclusion he'd reached earlier and, for Jonathan's sake, she was pleased.

'How did you get to know him?'

'He asked me to dance.'

'Damn cheek. Why did you accept?'

'Why shouldn't I have accepted? Mark was dancing with Pamela Gresham.'

Peter had noticed Mark and his partner closely entwined. He harrumphed. 'Then what? Did Drummond pester you?'

'Certainly not. When the dance ended he said goodnight and walked away.'

Aware that the mention of the blonde had made her fiancé uncomfortable, and remembering how he'd tried to bully Jonathan, Loris added with a touch of malice, 'I wouldn't have seen him again if Mark hadn't had to do his good deed for the evening…'

'Good deed? What good deed?'

Trying just a shade too hard to sound convincing, Mark told the same tale he'd told Isobel.

'It was Alan Gresham's daughter…she suddenly felt faint… There wasn't a taxi available at that minute, so I offered to drive her home. Unfortunately I couldn't find Loris to tell her.'

'It was after they'd gone,' Loris went on to explain, 'and Jonathan saw me standing in the rain, that he came up and offered me a lift.'

Knowing his future son-in-law, Peter—who was no fool and could read between the lines—decided to let the subject drop. He and Mark, with the same attitude to women, shared a man-to-man relationship.

Knowing Loris, he was satisfied he'd been wrong. She wasn't the kind to play games with a man she'd only just met.

He threw a couple of logs on the fire and, turning to Mark, began to talk business. 'When things have settled down and are running smoothly, I've decided to come into the office less. Once or twice a week should be enough.'

'You mean you'll be working from home, or letting go of the reins?'

'Gradually letting go of the reins. I'll be sixty-one soon, and I'd like to give more time to running the estate…'

Watching the two men, Loris could only be thankful that, in spite of making a complete fool of herself and deserving to pay for it, she seemed to have got off lightly and she and Mark were back on good terms.

Now all that remained was to forget about Jonathan and his brief intrusion into her life, and put the whole thing behind her.

She only hoped that he would have the sense to go back to the States. Though Mark had given his word not to hound him, the two men were so antipathetic to each other that if they came into contact they were bound to clash.

And next time Jonathan would undoubtedly come off worst.

She wouldn't think of Jonathan any more.

But having decided that, and in spite of all her efforts, for the rest of the afternoon and throughout dinner she found herself unable to think of anything but him.

Later, when she reluctantly agreed to fill in at bridge, her mind wasn't on the game, and she made so many mistakes that she was thankful Mark, rather than one of the other guests, was her partner.

When the rubber ended, and the men drifted towards the billiard table, instead of joining the ladies for a chat in the living-room she picked a book from the shelves at random and sat by the library fire.

Though well written, it failed to grip her and after a while the click of the billiard balls became soporific and, her head nodding in the warmth, her eyelids gradually drooped.

Half-asleep and half-awake, her wayward thoughts returned to Jonathan.

She could see his face as clearly as if he was standing there. His well-shaped head and clear-cut features, the way his thickly lashed green eyes crinkled at the corners when he smiled his charming, slightly lopsided smile, his chiselled lips and the firm chin with its intriguing cleft...

But it wasn't only how he *looked* that pleased and beguiled her, it was the man himself. His quiet strength and assurance, his awareness, his sense of humour and warmth.

She recalled the night spent in his arms, how his generosity and his obvious pleasure in her had carried her to the heights, how easily the passion and sweetness of his lovemaking had elicited an answering passion.

By removing a deep-rooted fear and restoring her faith in herself as a woman he had given her a precious gift, and she would be grateful to him for the rest of her days.

It was very largely that fear that had made her reluctant to commit herself to an earlier wedding date. But now she could go ahead and marry Mark without worrying that she might fail him as a wife, so some good had come out of her lapse...

'You look ready for bed.' Mark's voice broke into her thoughts.

Looking up, she saw that the game of billiards had ended and the men were clustered round the small bar, helping themselves to a nightcap.

'I am,' she said, and got to her feet.

'I'll walk you up.'

'Aren't you having a nightcap with the others?' she asked, knowing he usually had a whisky and soda.

'I'm not bothered.'

As they climbed the stairs he remarked, 'You've been very quiet all evening.' Then, a shade uneasily, 'Are you all right?'

It was unusual for Mark to ask such a question, and, touched, she answered, 'Fine. Just tired.'

At the door of her room, he asked, 'Can I come in? Or was that remark about being tired simply to warn me off?'

'No, it wasn't. It happens to be true.'

'So can I come in or not?'

Intending to say yes, she found herself saying, 'I'd rather you didn't.'

'Damn it, Loris, we're getting married as soon as it can be arranged. Anyone would think you didn't *want* me to make love to you...'

How could she let one man make love to her while her head was full of thoughts of another?

'Tonight I really hoped you'd say yes.'

'I'm sorry Mark, I *can't*.'

Picking up her desperation, and looking slightly embarrassed, he said, 'Oh... Oh, I see. Then perhaps I will have that nightcap after all.'

He kissed her with a marked lack of passion, and retreated down the stairs.

Rather than feeling guilty because she'd innocently misled him into thinking it was the wrong time of the month for her, all she could feel was relief as she prepared for bed.

But she couldn't go on like this, she lectured herself crossly. She really *must* put Jonathan right out of her head before thoughts of him compromised her future with Mark.

Over the next few days Loris discovered that was easier said than done. Though on her return to town she had made a strenuous effort not to think about Jonathan, whenever she relaxed her guard he simply walked in and took over.

He even came between her and her work. When, gazing at a wall with rapt attention, she should have been visualising colour schemes, all she could see in her mind's eye was his face.

Worse still was the treacherous way that her mind and body conspired together. Memories of the night they had spent together would sneak past her defences and filter into her consciousness, and her newly awakened body would react by growing heated and languorous and longing for his.

On Thursday, she paid a morning visit to a client with a mews cottage not far from Piccadilly. Vexed by her inability to concentrate, she decided to have lunch before going on to her mid-afternoon appointment at Bayswater.

After several days of lowering skies and periodic heavy downpours, it was raining steadily again as Loris hurried along Shear Lane. Furling her umbrella, she dived down the basement steps and into Il Lupo.

'Buon giorno.' She was greeted by the rotund and smil-

ing white-aproned owner, who hung up her mac and disposed of her umbrella before showing her to a small table in an alcove.

In common with the others it had a red-checked table-cloth, a lighted candle stuck in a wine bottle, and a plastic-covered menu in the red, white and green of the Italian flag.

She was gazing unseeingly at the menu, recalling the delicious chicken and pasta bake she had shared with Jonathan, when, as though her thoughts had conjured him up, a familiar voice said, 'Well, hello! I decided to have lunch here in the hope of seeing you.'

Wearing a smart grey business suit and a matching shirt and tie, he was standing smiling down at her.

Her heart gave a strange lurch and her breathing quickened. Despite his wet hair he looked well turned out, and even more handsome than she remembered.

As she gazed up at him, her golden eyes registering shock, he asked, 'May I join you?'

Apparently taking her silence for assent, he sat down opposite.

'No,' she begged belatedly, 'please don't. I promised Mark I wouldn't see you again.'

'Well, I made no such promise,' he said, a glint in his eye, 'so you can put the blame on me.'

Seeing all too clearly what kind of mood he was in, Loris considered getting up and leaving.

But, finding herself strangely unwilling to walk away, she said weakly, 'If Mark finds out he'll be very angry... I wish you'd go.'

'Go? I've only just come. I haven't had any lunch yet.'

'Then why don't you sit somewhere else? There's plenty of space.'

'If he found out that we were both in the same restaurant,

do you seriously think my sitting at the next table would
make him any less angry?'

Knowing he was right, she admitted, 'No. That's why
I'd like you to go. It's not safe.'

Dropping his voice to a gravelly, Humphrey Bogart rasp,
Jonathan leaned towards her and, almost without moving
his lips, asked, 'Is he having you followed, doll?'

Biting back a smile, she said, 'Of course he isn't having
me followed.'

'Then how will he know? Or do you feel compelled to
tell him?'

'No, I don't feel *compelled* to tell him, but I don't want
anything else on my conscience.'

He shook his head gloomily. 'Heavy enough, is it?'

'If you must know, it is!'

'Oh, well, in that case it might make more sense to tell
him. Confession's good for the soul.'

'If you'd only go,' she begged, 'there'd be nothing to
tell him.'

'It could already be too late,' Jonathan said dramatically.
'The office is only a few blocks away. He might be homing
in on Il Lupo right now, intent on having lunch.'

'You must be joking! Mark lunches at the Ritz. He
wouldn't be seen dead in a place like this.'

'Well, if he's not likely to walk in at any moment why
are you so jumpy?'

When she said nothing, looking at the open menu, he
asked blandly, 'I take it you haven't ordered yet?'

Throwing in the towel, she admitted, 'No.'

'Then may I suggest the *farsumagru*? I noticed it on the
"Today's Specials" board. If it's as good as I used to have
in Sardinia, I think you'll like it.'

'What is it exactly?'

'A kind of stuffed meat roll, with eggs and cheese and
herbs.'

Loris nodded her agreement, and when a young black-haired waiter appeared at his elbow Jonathan ordered *farsumagru* for them both, and a carafe of red wine.

Thinking it would be safer to steer clear of personal topics, and noting his mention of Sardinia, Loris remarked, 'The other night you said you'd done some travelling?'

'Yes. Before I settled in the States I spent a while taking a look at some of the world's more out-of-the-way places.'

'Such as?'

He named a few, and until their meal arrived kept her well entertained with stories and anecdotes about the people he'd met and the sometimes strange things that had happened.

The *farsumagru* was every bit as good as he'd suggested it might be, and for a while they ate in silence. Then, taking a sip of her wine, Loris asked, 'Are you a born traveller? Do you still get itchy feet?'

'I enjoy an occasional trip, but on the whole I'm more of a home bird than a traveller.' Ironically, he added, 'As conscience is said to make cowards of us, so unrequited love can make travellers of us. I guess it's the need to try and escape the pain.'

'Unrequited?' She found herself echoing the word. It was strange to think of any woman he had loved not loving him back. But though he'd spoken lightly, as if he were joking, for some reason she felt sure he wasn't.

He shrugged his shoulders. 'I wasn't good enough for her... However, that was a long time ago.'

But there must have been plenty of women since then—recalling his experienced and skilful lovemaking, she went hot all over, and a little shiver ran through her—or maybe just one special woman?

Only too aware that she should let the subject drop, she still found herself asking, 'So are you married now?'

'No.'

'And no plans to?'

'Oh, yes, I have plans…'

Though she knew she was being dog-in-a-manger, his answer gave her no pleasure.

Watching her face, he added, 'I'm having to work on them. Regrettably, the woman of my dreams—the woman I'm hoping to marry—is involved with someone else at the moment.'

She waited to see if he would elaborate further.

He didn't. Instead, he asked, 'Is your wedding still on?'

'Of course it's still on.'

'I was hoping you'd changed your mind. Longton isn't the man for you. He doesn't know you. And he's far too selfish to even understand let alone *fulfil*, your needs—'

Because what he was saying disturbed her, she broke in sharply, 'What makes you so sure? Mark and I have known each other for months. It's *you* who doesn't know me.'

His gaze steady, he objected, 'I should say that in one sense I know you a great deal better than he does.'

Her eyes fell, and despite all her efforts she felt herself starting to blush.

Watching the tide of colour rise in her cheeks, Jonathan added, 'Unless, your doubts about being frigid now removed, you've spent the last two or three nights in his bed. Have you, Loris?'

She hadn't intended to answer, but as though he'd willed the truth out of her she found herself saying, 'No, I haven't.'

His faint sigh of relief was audible.

'But don't get the wrong idea,' she added firmly, 'I *am* going to marry him. It's all arranged.'

There was a short pause. Then, as though accepting the inevitable, he asked, 'So when is the wedding to take place?'

'A week tomorrow.' Realising how flat her voice sounded, she smiled brilliantly.

Frowning, he said, 'As soon as that? Is it to be a church wedding?'

She shook her head. 'Register office. Mother's bitterly disappointed, but, having been divorced, Mark wants to keep the whole thing very quiet, no fuss.'

Jonathan raised a well-marked brow. 'No honeymoon either?'

'No. At least not until the summer.'

'What are you doing about your job?'

'Working until a couple of days before the wedding.'

'Then what?'

'I'll be carrying on at least until June, as Mark and I agreed.'

'I thought he might have managed to talk you out of it?'

'He's tried,' she admitted. 'But after we're married he wants to live in the house his parents left him—a house that's fully staffed. I can't begin to imagine how I'd fill my time. Perhaps it won't be so bad when we start a family,' she added hopefully.

'Then you want children?'

'Yes.'

'Does Longton?'

'Of course.'

'What makes you so sure?'

'When I told him I'd like children, he said he would too.'

'That surprises me.'

'Why should it surprise you?'

His green eyes holding no warmth, his voice brittle as ice, Jonathan observed, 'Well, he doesn't show much interest in the one he's got.'

'What?' she asked blankly.

Jonathan repeated his observation.

'I don't know what you mean. He and his first wife didn't have any children.'

'He and his *wife* might not have had any, but his ex-fiancée certainly does—'

Her jaw dropped. 'His *ex-fiancée*?'

'The one you supplanted.'

With certainty, she said, 'I didn't supplant anyone. The whole idea's ridiculous! Mark had no ties when I met him.'

'How do you know?'

'He said so.'

'And you believed him?'

'Why shouldn't I have believed him? He had nothing to hide. He told me about his divorce—'

'That was common knowledge, so he was forced to. But did he tell you *why* his wife divorced him?'

'They were incompatible. They found it impossible to live together.'

'I understood that the thing she found impossible to live with was his penchant for other women.'

'I'm quite aware that Mark likes women, but that's so with a lot of men, and it doesn't mean he'll do anything about it when we're married. I'm also aware that women find *him* attractive.'

'And you're prepared to live with that?'

Challenged, she said, 'Maybe I wouldn't want a man that no other women would bother to look twice at.'

'I gather his first wife didn't feel that way. Fortunately, or *unfortunately*, however you care to look at it, and possibly because she *was* his wife, she was by no means as reconciled to his numerous affairs as the woman who came after her.'

'I don't believe he had "numerous affairs" while he was married, and he told me he hadn't had a relationship until he met me since he and his wife separated.'

'How long did you say you'd been engaged?' Jonathan asked abruptly. 'Three months, was it?'

'Yes.'

'Then while he was putting a ring on *your* finger, your predecessor—whom he'd earlier promised to marry—was in a private nursing home awaiting the birth of their baby.'

Aghast, Loris whispered. 'No, you *must* be mistaken! When we've talked about children Mark's never breathed a word about having any. And there hasn't been so much as a whisper...'

'He's managed to keep it very quiet. In fact I doubt if anyone, including your father, has the faintest inkling.'

Loris lifted her chin and looked him in the eye. 'You've only been over from the States a few weeks, so how did *you* get to know all this?'

'For reasons which I'd prefer not to go into I don't want to disclose my source. However, I can assure you that it's absolutely true.'

Flatly she said, 'I'm sorry, but I don't believe a word of it. Mark has his faults—he's arrogant, quick-tempered, and he can be insensitive at times—but he isn't the kind to behave as callously as you're trying to make out.'

'I'm not "trying to make out" anything. I'm simply giving you the facts as I know them.'

'Well, I'm sure you've been misinformed. And as you don't want to tell me where you got hold of these *facts*, I'll continue to regard the whole thing as a complete fabrication.'

'Use your common sense, Loris. Why should anyone make up a story like that?'

'I can't imagine,' she said shortly. 'Unless it's someone with a grudge against Mark, someone who's just out to stir up trouble.'

Recalling how much animosity there was between the two men, and wondering how pure Jonathan's own motives were, she asked, 'Why did you make it your business to tell me?'

'I thought you should know about this other woman. She knows about you... Oh, no, Longton didn't tell her. She read about your engagement in the papers. I must say I'm rather surprised he agreed to have it put in.'

'Well, he did. Anyway, if this "other woman" knows about me, why hasn't she kicked up a fuss?'

'I understand that he supports her quite generously, but on the understanding that she keeps her mouth shut and stays in the background. For the sake of their child, and because, in spite of everything, she still loves him and lives in hopes of getting him back on a *permanent* basis, she's prepared to put up with it.'

'Are you saying he still sees her?'

'Oh, yes, he visits her a couple of times a week.'

'I don't believe it. Why should any woman allow herself to be treated so shabbily?'

'Because, though he had other women while they were together, he swore they meant nothing to him, that it was *her* he loved, and she's fool enough to believe him...'

Disconcerted, Loris wondered. Suppose the story was true? But if it *was*, and he'd had any feelings for the woman who was the mother of his child, surely he would have married her rather than propose to someone else?

Slowly, she said, 'Just for the sake of argument, if he had a cosy little set-up, where this woman was willing to ignore his affairs, why should he have asked me to marry him?'

'My guess—and this *is* just a guess—is that he saw you, *wanted* you, and, because of *who you are*, and because you weren't easy like the rest, he decided he'd have to marry you to get what he wanted. Also, being married to Sir Peter Bergman's daughter will give him a certain standing, an added prestige, as well as keeping the business in the family.'

Jonathan's reasoning was plausible and, shaken despite herself, Loris avoided those clear green eyes that saw too much.

Looking at her downbent face, he asked gently, 'You honestly believe he loves you?'

'He said he did.'

'I'd be surprised if he can even spell the word,' Jonathan said caustically. He added, 'His mistress may try to delude herself that he still loves her—though I don't know how she can after the way he's treated her—but that kind of man is incapable of loving anyone but himself.'

He sounded so bitter, so *concerned*, that Loris found herself wondering whether this woman might possibly be the one Jonathan wanted to marry. Though if it was true that she'd been having a long-term affair with Mark, it did seem unlikely.

Taking a deep breath, she asked, 'What about the child? You say Mark has a child?'

'Yes, he has a baby daughter. A daughter that he almost totally ignores.'

Loris was shocked. Even if he had no feelings for the mother, how could any man ignore his own child?

As though reading her thoughts, Jonathan advised quietly, 'Before you decide to go ahead with the wedding, it might be as well to ask yourself what kind of husband and father a man like him is going to make... Unless you're afraid of the answer?'

His question had the smooth abrasiveness of pumice-stone, and suddenly she knew without a shadow of doubt that, for whatever reason, he didn't want her to marry Mark.

Her earlier suspicion that he was simply out to make trouble returned in a rush. She took a deep breath. 'You said you'd decided to lunch here in the hope of seeing me...'

His eyes on her face, he waited silently.

'Why? Was it just so you could tell me this story about Mark having a mistress and a child?'

'You sound accusing. Would you rather have gone ahead with the wedding without knowing?'

She shook her head. 'No, I suppose not.'

If it *was* the truth she did want to know... Though she was sure it *wasn't*, she reminded herself hastily.

But, whether it was true or not, she guessed that he'd told her purposely, in order to blacken Mark's character and throw a spanner in the works.

She was oddly disappointed. Somehow it seemed unworthy of him.

Hoping he would refute the suggestion, she asked, 'I take it this is your way of trying to get back at Mark?'

'You could say that,' Jonathan admitted. 'Though probably not for the reason you imagine.'

Angry and disillusioned now—she hadn't put him down as petty or vindictive—she gave him a look of cold hostility. 'For whatever reason, I think it's despicable to try to poison my mind against him.'

Pushing back her chair, she jumped to her feet and made for the door. Grabbing her mac *en route*, she struggled into it and, fumbling with her umbrella, almost ran up the basement steps.

Rain was still pouring from a sky nearly as dark as night. The pavement shone wet and gleaming in the lights; the gutters ran with water.

She had gone only a short distance when it occurred to her that she had rushed off without paying the bill. Her steps faltered and she half turned.

Then, changing her mind, unwilling to face Jonathan

again, she hurried on. Let *him* pay. He'd had his money's worth—discrediting Mark, upsetting her, and in the process destroying what had been her growing respect for him.

Strangely enough, the latter mattered most of all.

CHAPTER SIX

LORIS had reached the far end of Shear Lane and was waiting to cross the road when Jonathan suddenly appeared by her side. He was bare-headed, the collar of his stone-coloured mac turned up against the rain.

The lights changed. Calmly taking charge of her umbrella, his other hand beneath her elbow, he crossed with her.

Picking up the conversation as though there had been no interruption, he said, 'I wasn't trying to poison your mind, merely open your eyes. As I told you the night we met, Longton isn't a very nice character.'

'And as I told you, that's a matter of opinion. At least he doesn't go sneaking behind people's backs...and he's honest enough to admit when he's in the wrong.'

'Would you call hiding the fact that he has a mistress and a child honest?'

Jerking her elbow free, she retorted curtly, 'As it happens, I don't believe a word of it.'

'Then when you see him tonight try asking him.'

But when his afternoon meeting ended Mark was flying to the Continent on business. He wouldn't be back until tomorrow night. Suddenly she knew that was much too long to wait.

Impatient to get at the truth, to hear Mark refute the allegation once and for all, she said, 'We're quite close to the offices, and he should be back from lunch any time, so why not ask him now?'

'Why not, indeed? And don't forget to watch his face while you're asking him.'

But, already starting to anticipate one difficulty, she pointed out, 'The problem is, he's bound to want to know where I heard such a story.'

'Feel free to tell him.'

Although she was upset and angry with Jonathan, she couldn't do that. It would be as good as signing his death warrant.

'No, I…I don't want to tell him. It would only cause a great deal of trouble.'

'You mean he'd find some way to dismiss me? Don't worry about that.'

'I don't want you to lose your job through me.'

'That's heartening,' he said ironically. 'Judging by the inimical look you gave me earlier, anyone would have thought a firing squad was too good for me.'

'Well, what else can you expect? You slander the man I…' about to say *love* she changed it to, 'I'm going to marry—'

Stopping in his tracks, Jonathan turned towards her. Still holding the orange umbrella sprinkled with white daisies over her head, he took her chin between the finger and thumb of his free hand and made her look at him.

His hair dark and dripping, rain running down his face, he said quietly, 'You're wrong on at least one of those counts, and I hope on both. Slander is a *false* statement, and everything I told you was true. Though I dislike and disapprove of men like Longton, it gave me no pleasure to have to do what I just did. But it was necessary to put you in the picture before it was too late.'

More shaken than she cared to admit, she jeered, 'So you regard it as your mission in life to stop me marrying Mark? Well, if I need a knight in shining armour, I'll let you know.'

Jerking free, she carried on walking. 'Otherwise I'd like

it if you'd mind your own business and stay out of my life.'

Keeping pace with her, he said solemnly, 'I'm not sure I can do that.'

With an odd kind of flutter, she demanded, 'Why not?'

He sighed. 'Well, it would be such a waste.'

She glanced sideways at him. 'You mean if I marry Mark?'

'Not exactly.'

'Then what *do* you mean?'

'Well, apart from the fact that you owe me a lunch, I've just bought a new tin of metal polish.'

It was indicative of her state of mind that it took her a second or two to catch on. He meant he was already her knight in shining armour!

Gritting her teeth and staring straight ahead, she walked even faster.

In less than a minute they had reached the elegant old building that housed the BLC offices, and were mounting the steps with a straggle of staff just returning from lunch.

Though most people were stopping just clear of the doors to wipe their feet, the marble floor of the large lobby was wet from dripping macs and umbrellas. Jonathan shook and furled Loris's umbrella, and presented it to her gravely.

Dropping it into one of the troughs provided for visitors, she thanked him, her voice cold.

Mark's suite of offices was on the top floor, next door to her father's, and she was halfway to the lifts when, a hand on her arm, Jonathan stopped her. 'Aren't you for-getting something?'

'Of course,' she said acidly, 'I'm so sorry.' She fumbled in her shoulder-bag for her purse. 'I still owe you for lunch.'

He stopped her. 'That wasn't quite what I had in mind.' Green eyes looked steadily into amber. 'A civil goodbye would have been nice...' Glancing across the lobby, he added, 'But now circumstances favour something a little more demonstrative.'

Before she could begin to guess his intention he cupped both her elbows and, drawing her towards him, covered her mouth with his.

Taken by surprise, she made no attempt to struggle, merely stood there, acquiescent, while he kissed her lightly but proprietorially, making her heart start to race and the world tilt on its axis.

As he released her and stepped back, leaving her face wet from the contact with his, she looked up dazedly to see Mark standing stock-still just inside the entrance, glaring in their direction.

His expression made it plain that he'd seen the little incident, and she knew without a shadow of a doubt that he'd been *meant* to.

Before she could begin to regain her equilibrium, a man she recognised as William Grant, one of Cosby's top executives, walked past.

Noticing Jonathan, he paused. 'If you could spare a moment, Mr Drummond? There's something I need to ask you about before the afternoon meeting.'

'Of course. Would you like to come up to my office?' Smiling at Loris, Jonathan added pleasantly, '*Au revoir*, Miss Bergman.'

Still feeling stunned, knocked off balance, she watched the two men carry on towards the lifts.

A moment later, his face black as a thundercloud, Mark was looming over her. Seizing hold of her wrist, he demanded in a furious undertone, 'Damn it, Loris, are you *trying* to provoke me?'

'Of course not. I—'

'You promised you wouldn't see Drummond again. Next thing I know you're kissing him, not only in public, but right under my very nose. What the hell do you think you're playing at?'

'Mark, let go of my wrist!'

His grip tightened even more. 'Well, answer my question.'

'Let her go.' Jonathan's voice, though quiet, cracked like a whip.

Startled, Mark exclaimed, 'Why, you—!'

'Do as I say, unless you want to end up flat on your back with everyone looking on.'

Letting go of Loris's wrist, Mark turned on his adversary, his big hands clenched into fists of rage. 'Don't be a fool, man,' Jonathan said in the same quiet, even tone. 'There's no point in making a scene.'

'What's the matter? Scared?' Mark taunted.

'Not at all.' His voice matter-of-fact, Jonathan added, 'But I don't want to be involved in a fracas unless I'm forced. I've never cared for violence. However, if you lay another finger on Loris I'll be tempted to forget my scruples and break your neck. Is that clear? Oh, and in answer to your question, she wasn't "playing at" anything. Loris didn't kiss *me*. *I* kissed *her*. She had no choice in the matter, and is totally blameless. So if you want to take it out on anyone, it will have to be me.'

That wasn't strictly true, Loris was forced to admit. She could have pulled away, she could have smacked his face, but she'd done neither. Like someone under a spell, she had just stood there and let him kiss her. Enjoyed it even. She hastily snapped off the disloyal thought.

'Now, if you'll excuse me,' Jonathan went on, 'William Grant is waiting for me.' Over his shoulder he added, 'But don't forget what I said.'

His lips drawn back over strong white teeth, Mark snarled, 'Of all the arrogant, overweening young upstarts—'

'Please, Mark,' Loris interrupted with a touch of desperation, 'let's go up to your office. We can't talk standing here in the lobby.'

Without a word, but obviously still seething, he turned and headed across to the lifts.

Thankful they were leaving, Loris followed him.

She breathed a sigh of relief to find that there was no sign of Jonathan and William Grant amongst the little knot of people waiting. The last thing she wanted was for them all to be forced to ride up together.

When she and Mark got out of the lift on the top floor, they walked a yard or two along a wide corridor before turning the corner to his suite of offices.

As he led the way through the outer office, Mark gave his grey-haired secretary curt instructions that they weren't to be disturbed.

Obviously well used to him, she enquired calmly, 'You haven't forgotten you have a meeting in your office at two-thirty?'

'No, I haven't forgotten,' he snapped, before leading the way into the inner sanctum.

Mark's huge office was luxuriously carpeted and furnished, with an imposing desk and a built-in bar. Displayed in a glass case were several cups and trophies, and a series of first-class sporting prints adorned the walls.

By this time reaction had set in. Feeling distinctly shaky, Loris dropped her bag, pulled off her mac, and took a seat in one of the big leather armchairs. Mark—perhaps because it gave him back his feeling of authority—chose to sit behind his desk.

On his desk top, along with all the latest technology, was a picture of Loris.

She was oddly touched to see it there.

Before she could decide just how to begin, he said brusquely, his heavy face set and angry, 'You'd better start by telling me why you broke your promise not to see Drummond again.'

Sounding cooler than she actually was, she said, 'I didn't break my promise. Well, not on purpose...'

'Then what were you two doing together?'

'I'd decided to have lunch before going on to my next appointment. I was looking at the menu when he suddenly appeared and sat down at my table.'

'Out of the whole of London, he just happened to choose the same restaurant? What a remarkable coincidence!' Mark said incredulously.

'It wasn't exactly a coincidence,' she admitted. 'While he was at Monkswood I mentioned that when I was in town I often lunched at Il Lupo, as it was good and cheap... And of course it's quite close to here.'

'So he went there purposely, hoping to see you?'

Instinctively trying to save Jonathan's skin, she lied, 'I can't say whether he went purposely or not. Maybe it just happened...'

'So when you'd shared a nice cosy lunch, you couldn't bear to leave him?'

'No... I left the restaurant first. I was waiting to cross Shear Lane when he caught up with me, and we walked the rest of the way here together.'

'Why did you come *here* rather than going on to your next appointment?'

'I wanted to see you. I need to talk to you.'

'And whatever it is couldn't have waited until tomorrow night?'

'No, it couldn't,' she said flatly. 'It's important.'

Unconvinced, he brushed her assurance aside, and went back to his interrogation. 'So what the devil was Drummond doing mauling you about?'

Though his kiss had rocked her, she remembered the

lightness of it, the finesse, and she objected, 'I'd hardly call it "mauling me about"'...'

Mark's scowl told her she was making things worse.

In an effort to be more conciliatory, she explained, 'I was leaving him, intending to come up to your office, when he stopped me. He said I'd walked away without even saying goodbye. That's when he...he kissed me.'

'He wasn't afraid I'd see him?'

'Quite the opposite,' she said drily. Then wanted to kick herself.

Mark cottoned on immediately. 'You mean he'd seen me come in, and he did it on purpose to annoy me?'

'I'm afraid so.'

'Well, believe me, he'll live to regret it... After the way he tried to make a fool of me in front of quite a number of the staff—'

'I thought he was trying to stop you making a fool of yourself.' Realising she'd been less than diplomatic, Loris wished she'd guarded her unruly tongue.

'Of course you would have to stick up for that swine,' Mark said harshly.

'I'm not sticking up for him. But remember you promised that, no matter what, you wouldn't take any action against him. That was why I agreed to bring the wedding forward.'

His face tense, he demanded, 'You're not backing out now, just because of Drummond?'

Knowing there was little else she could do until Mark had calmed down, and reminding herself that Jonathan had asked for everything he'd got, she said, 'No, I'm not backing out. But I would like you to keep your side of the bargain.'

Noting more than a hint of relief mingling with the anger in his brown eyes, she added, 'Please, Mark, can't we let the matter drop and get onto what I came for?'

He moved his heavy shoulders in an irritable gesture. 'Very well. You said it was important, so I suppose it's something to do with the arrangements for the wedding?'

'Not exactly.' She swallowed. 'You told me that after you and your wife split up you didn't have a relationship until I came along.'

When he said nothing, she added, 'Is that true?'

His expression closed, he said, 'Yes, it is.'

'You didn't get engaged to anyone else?'

'Engaged? Certainly not.'

'But you lived with someone?'

'Look, what are you getting at?'

'I heard there was another woman in your life—'

'*You* are, and have been, the only woman I've had a relationship with since my marriage broke up.' Then, quickly, 'If you're thinking of Pamela, I'd never even set eyes on her before the party. She was just a one-night stand, and you know quite well why. You're not still holding that against me?'

'No, this has nothing to do with Pamela.'

Sounding impatient now, he asked, 'Then what has it to do with?'

'I heard that after your wife left you lived with someone else, and that she had a baby by you.'

'*What?*' He jumped to his feet. 'Where in hell's name did you hear a preposterous story like that?'

'Where I heard it isn't important. Is it true?'

'Of course it isn't true!' Mark looked so upset she believed him straight away. She told herself she felt relieved and her face softened. 'I'm sorry, Mark.'

He shook his head and replied, 'I don't blame you for thinking the worst of me—especially after Pamela. But I've learnt my lesson. I may have been a bit too easily led when it came to the opposite sex in the past, but when we're married I swear I won't so much as *look* at another woman.

You're all I've ever wanted, and with you in my bed, and a family of my own, I'll be the happiest man in the world.'

Before she could reply, he came around the desk and kissed her. When he pulled back and smiled at her, Loris told herself that his speech was all that she could have wanted, and that she was doing the right thing in marrying him. But she couldn't help feeling slightly uneasy at the memory of Jonathan's earnest face as he'd told her of Mark's supposed mistress and child. He'd almost convinced her!

Breaking into her thoughts, Mark asked, 'Where did you hear about this, anyway? I'd very much like to know.'

Shaking her head, she said, 'It doesn't matter.'

'It matters to me. Damn it, Loris, *who* told you? Whoever dug it up was clearly just trying to make trouble.'

Watching his big frame stiffen, she knew he had guessed the truth.

'*Drummond!* Who else? It was him, wasn't it? I ought to have realised at once... Well, this time he'll find he's definitely overstepped the mark. I'll show him who's boss. I'll get him sacked if it's the last thing I do!'

Loris bit her lip. Though she didn't believe Jonathan's story, she thought he did. The person who'd fed him the lies could well have been one of the business enemies Mark had made in the past, trying to discredit him with Cosby's. Yes, that was the most likely explanation—so it wasn't really Jonathan's fault.

Only too aware that it was touch and go, and she'd have to tread carefully, she said, without undue emphasis, 'Don't you think you might be jumping to conclusions? Allowing yourself to be prejudiced?'

'You mean it *wasn't* Drummond?'

'Is it likely he'd know a thing like that when he's only been over from the States a short time?'

'Well, if it wasn't him, who the devil was it?'

'As I've already said, it doesn't matter.'

Seeing he looked far from happy at being put off, she smiled at him. 'And I know the truth, so, rather than keep talking about it, I'd much sooner forget the whole thing.'

Anxious to get away before he pressed her any further, she reminded him, 'Haven't you a meeting scheduled for two-thirty?'

'Yes.' He glanced at his watch. 'They'll be here any minute.'

'Then I'd better go.'

He took her in his arms again and smiled down at her, his face transformed by charm. It was easy to see why so many women fell for him.

She felt a stirring of the old excitement, the kind of attraction that had first drawn her to him, and when he kissed her she kissed him back with an enthusiasm she hadn't displayed recently.

'That's much more like it,' he said with satisfaction, and kissed her again, enjoying the warmth of her response.

In just over a week they would be married, she thought with a little glow, and once they were man and wife, the tension that of late had soured their relationship should soon disappear. They would be at ease with one another, free to enjoy their future together...

Mark drew back with a sigh, and, glancing at the couch, said ruefully, 'It's a great pity about that meeting, but I'm afraid it's far too late to cancel it.'

Flustered, blushing a little at the thought of making love in his office, she pulled on her mac, gathered up her bag, and headed for the door.

Her hand was on the doorknob, when he said, 'If the flight's on time, I'll be round at your place about six-thirty tomorrow evening.'

'Fine.' She turned to smile at him and blow him a kiss before closing the door behind her.

She was still smiling when she reached the end of the corridor and turned towards the lifts.

The smile died from her lips when she saw Jonathan, his eyes on her face, leaning nonchalantly against the wall opposite. He had dried off, she noticed, and his hair, once more smoothly brushed, had returned to its normal fairness.

Oddly disconcerted by his presence, she asked crossly, 'Have you nothing better to do than lie in wait for me?'

His eyebrows shot up. 'You think I was lying in wait for you?'

'Yes. Otherwise what would you be doing lurking in the corridor?'

'Would you believe it if I told you I'm *en route* to join a meeting in Longton's office?'

Made suspicious by the way the question was phrased, she demanded, 'Are you?'

'I'm supposed to be.' Shamelessly, he added, 'Though I must admit that my real object *was* to lie in wait for you and find out how things had gone.'

Pressing the call button for the lift, she said haughtily, 'Well, as I've no intention of telling you, perhaps you'd better get on your way rather than waste the firm's time.'

A gleam in his green eyes, he mocked, 'You're starting to sound just like the boss's daughter.'

'I *am* the boss's daughter,' she reminded him tartly as the lift sighed to a halt and the doors slid open.

It was empty, and without a backward glance she stepped inside.

Jonathan followed close on her heels.

'I thought you were supposed to be going to the meeting,' she said sharply, as he reached to touch one of the buttons.

'There are more important things in life than attending meetings.'

Drily, she observed, 'I just hope Mr Grant agrees with you.'

'I'm sure he will. He's a good man, and on most things we're in complete accord. He'll back me all the way.'

'For your sake, I hope so.'

'Does that mean Longton's gunning for me?'

'It means you can't afford to take any *more* risks.' As she finished speaking the lift sighed to a stop and the doors slid open.

Eager to escape, Loris was halfway out when she realised that they were on the second floor, rather than in the foyer.

Before she could dig her toes in Jonathan had thrown a firm arm around her waist, swept her across the corridor, through a door opposite, and into a small, functional office, the antithesis of Mark's.

'What are you doing?' she cried, pulling free. 'I haven't got time to play silly games.'

'It wasn't silly games I had in mind. More a serious talk.'

'I've an appointment in Bayswater at three-thirty,' she said coldly.

'That will give us ample time. I'll call you a taxi when we've finished.'

As she started to protest, he added smoothly, 'I'll even pay for it.'

He was standing between her and the door, and though his stance was casual she felt convinced he had no intention of letting her leave until he'd learnt what he wanted to know.

'Won't you sit down?' he suggested politely.

Her common sense insisted that he wasn't likely to manhandle her, and she toyed briefly with the idea of telling him to go to hell and simply walking out.

But, as though his will was stronger than hers, she found herself weakly taking a seat in one of the plastic-covered swivel chairs.

He came and sat on the corner of the desk, and, crossing his arms, asked, 'So how did it go?'

'How did what go?'

Ignoring her attempt to stonewall, he said, 'When you rounded that corner you were smiling.'

'There's no law against it.'

'You hardly looked like a woman who's just learnt her fiancé isn't to be trusted.'

'Perhaps that's because I hadn't learnt any such thing.'

'So you didn't ask him?'

'Yes, I did.'

'And he denied the whole thing?'

'I don't see that what went on between Mark and me is any of your business.'

'For reasons that I won't go into at the moment, I'm making it my business.'

When she sat stubbornly silent, he sighed. 'Oh, well, if *you* won't tell me what happened, I'll have to ask Longton.'

'Do you really think he'd tell you?' she demanded incredulously.

'He might see sense. But if I have no alternative I'm prepared to beat it out of him.'

That quietly spoken threat should have seemed ridiculous, but she had no doubt—not only that Jonathan *meant* what he said, but that he could *do* it.

She shuddered, before asking caustically, 'Wouldn't it be easier to beat it out of me?'

'I've never struck a woman in my life, and I've no intention of starting now. Though there are other more enjoyable ways...' All at once he was standing over her, his eyes on her mouth.

Panic-stricken at the thought of him kissing her, she cried, 'Don't! Don't you dare touch me... All right, I'll *tell* you...'

'Dear me,' he murmured mildly. 'If I'd realised what an effective approach that was I'd have used it earlier.'

'And I thought Mark was good at intimidation,' she said bitterly.

Jonathan's smile was grim. 'He might be good at intimidation, but, remembering how happy you looked when you left him, I strongly suspect he's better at lying.'

'I happen to believe him,' she said stoutly.

'If you'd care to tell me what he said, I'll be able to judge for myself.'

Reluctantly, she said, 'He denied it completely.'

'And you believe that load of clap-trap?' Jonathan asked incredulously. 'Use your brains, Loris. He's lied to you before and he's lying to you now.'

Back on the see-saw of doubt, and hating it, she jumped to her feet, forcing him to step back a pace.

'You're wasting your time,' she said coldly. 'And I'd much prefer it if in future you stopped trying to interfere in my life and kept your nose out of Mark's affairs. In fact it would be better all round if you went back to the States. Now, if you don't mind, I want to leave.'

'Would you like me to call you a taxi?'

'No, thank you.' Picking up her bag, she headed for the door.

CHAPTER SEVEN

JONATHAN easily got there first, and for a moment she thought he was going to prevent her leaving, but instead he reached to open the door for her.

'*Au revoir*, Miss Bergman.'

'*Goodbye*, Mr Drummond.'

'Oh, just one more thing...'

Like a fool, she paused and turned.

The door was promptly closed.

A split-second later her bag thudded to the floor, her arms were pinned to her sides, and his mouth was on hers.

This time she struggled hard, but he held her easily, effortlessly. When she attempted to kick his shins her feet were neatly hooked from beneath her, leaving her completely off balance.

At first his kiss was punitive, conveying only too clearly the anger he felt. But after a moment or two it gentled and turned into a series of soft, plucking baby-kisses, kisses that coaxed and beguiled and made her want to open her mouth to him.

Her lips pressed tightly together, she was trying to resist the temptation when, with a suddenness that caught her by surprise, he nipped her bottom lip between his teeth.

It was just hard enough to make her gasp, and he took instant advantage, deepening the kiss until the world reeled and heat surged through her body.

She was lost, mindless, when he lifted his head, and, setting her on her feet, bent to retrieve her bag and hand it to her.

An instant later there was a tap at the door, and it opened to admit one of the girls belonging to the junior staff.

Perhaps sensitive to atmosphere, she glanced curiously from one to the other. 'Sorry to disturb you, Mr Drummond, but Mr Grant asked me to remind you about the meeting.'

'Thank you, Caley. Please will you tell him I'll be along directly?'

As, looking as though she'd like to linger, the girl turned to go, Jonathan said to Loris, 'Well, I'll say *au revoir*, Miss Bergman. Many thanks for your time and help... Allow me to see you out.'

His obsequious manner was contradicted by the devilish gleam in his eyes.

Gritting her teeth, she stalked past him without a word and, too agitated to wait for the lift, took the stairs down to the foyer.

It was still raining hard, and, retrieving her umbrella, she set off through the downpour. At the corner she spotted a cruising taxi and flagged it down. It would be the last straw if she was late for her appointment.

It was after five when Loris got back to her flat. She felt unsettled and dispirited. Her appointment had proved to be disappointing, as it had soon become apparent that, rather than being serious about a commission, all the owner of the penthouse wanted was free advice. Which meant that the time she had put aside the following day to do preliminary sketches was now time wasted.

And, as if that wasn't bad enough, she had been unable to get Jonathan Drummond out of her head. Over and over again some mental video had replayed the afternoon's events.

The way he had forced her to confront Mark... The way he had defended her in the foyer... The way he had kissed her... The way he had succeeded in putting fresh doubts in her mind...

Not for the first time, she found herself wondering what he hoped to gain by throwing a spanner in the works.

It was clear that he disliked Mark and wanted to prevent her from marrying him. But *why*? There had to be more to it than mere dislike. Despite all that had passed between them, it couldn't be because he had any romantic interest in her. He'd admitted to having wedding plans of his own.

Thoroughly disgruntled, wishing she'd never set eyes on Jonathan Drummond, she went through to the kitchen to make herself a cup of tea. While she drank it, she listened to the messages on her answering machine.

The first one added to her gloom by cancelling an appointment she had made for the next day, and that was followed by several that were merely run-of-the-mill. Only the last one was of real interest. The caller was a Mrs Marchant who, having seen and admired some of Loris's work, wanted her to look over a small manor house near Fenny Oak.

After a brief description of the twelve-roomed property, the friendly-sounding voice went on, 'We've just recently bought Fenny Manor. It's only partially furnished, and the whole place has been badly neglected, so it all needs refurbishing. To be honest I've neither the time nor the talent for such a project, so we'd like to know as soon as possible whether you'd be interested? If you could fit in a visit tomorrow, or even better tonight, we'd be very grateful.

'By the way, money's no object, and if you did decide to accept the commission, you'd be given a completely free hand. Perhaps you'd let us know?'

She had left a telephone number.

It sounded exactly the kind of big, exciting project Loris had always hoped for, and being busy tonight would take her mind off other things.

Her spirits rising, she tapped in the digits, and after a couple of rings the same pleasant voice answered, 'Hello?'

'This is Loris Bergman.'

'Oh, Miss Bergman, it's very kind of you to call back so quickly. I'm only too aware of how short the notice is, so I dared hardly let myself hope you'd be free tomorrow.'

'As a matter of fact I can get over tonight,' Loris said.

'Oh, that's absolutely wonderful! But we're a little way out of London. I don't suppose you've ever heard of Fenny Oak? It's a small hamlet not very far from the village of Paddleham.'

'As a matter of fact I know the area. It's only a few miles from where my parents live.'

'Excellent. Do you happen to know Watersmeet? Well, Fenny Manor stands on the strip of higher ground between the River Fenny and the River Mere. It's the only house on the island, so you can't go wrong. At the bottom of Watersmeet Lane, which is signposted as a private road, there's an old stone bridge over the Fenny... You do have a car, by the way?'

'No, I don't. With most of my work being in London, and taking into account the traffic jams and the difficulties of parking, it's easier to use taxis.'

'Well, if you come by taxi we'll be more than happy to meet your expenses. Oh, and before I forget, the recent floods have weakened the bridge to the point where it may be unsafe for vehicles, so you'll need to ask the taxi to wait on the far side and walk over. But it's only a hundred yards or so to the house. If you can tell us roughly what time you expect to arrive, I'll watch out for you.'

Wondering when they had their evening meal, Loris asked, 'What time would suit you best? Seven-thirty? Or later perhaps?'

'Make it seven-thirty if you can, and if you've no other

plans why not have dinner with us? Get the feel of the place…'

'Thank you, that would be nice.'

It was a pitch-black night and the rain was still falling steadily as, just before seven-thirty, Loris's taxi drove through the picturesque hamlet of Fenny Oak and turned down Watersmeet Lane.

Their lights made a bright tunnel between bare hedges and waterlogged fields, and gleamed on the surface water that covered the roadway to a depth of several inches.

Prewarned on booking that it might entail waiting for a couple of hours or more, the driver, a chatty, middle-aged man who owned his own cab, had said with cheery unconcern, 'Don't worry, love, I'm used to it. It's all part of the job. A packet of sandwiches and a newspaper help to pass the time. And if I wasn't sitting waiting I'd be battling with the London evening traffic. So what's the odds?'

Now, as the road dipped, and the level of the water rose correspondingly, he said judiciously, 'Let's hope it doesn't get any deeper, or we might have a job getting back.'

They approached the end of the lane to find that it opened out onto a wide, cobblestoned area lit by two old-fashioned streetlamps.

A stone bridge crossed the river at this point and a little way beyond, set on higher ground, Loris could see the bulk of a house, its lighted windows a welcoming sight.

The River Fenny, little more than a gentle stream in the summer, was now swollen and fast-flowing. Its brown muddy water, swirling along branches and other storm debris, battered at the bridge supports and, filling the arch, surged against the old stonework.

Coming to a halt on rising ground that formed the approach to the bridge, the driver suggested, 'If you jump out here, you shouldn't get your feet wet.'

'Thanks. Sure you'll be OK? It won't be very warm, just sitting.'

'I'll be fine. If I do get chilly I can always run the engine a bit.'

Loris tightened the belt of her mac, pulled on her sou'wester-type rain hat, and stepped out into the downpour. Slamming the cab door behind her, she hurried across the bridge.

The force of the water seemed to shake its very foundations, and in the light from the lamps she could see where some of the mortar between the stones that formed the roadway was starting to crumble away. It was quite scary, and she was glad to get to the other side.

The drive, running between sloping green lawns, was paved and well-lit, and as she climbed the steps to the terrace a door opened, spilling golden light onto the flagstones.

A slim, attractive woman, about her own height, with grey eyes and fair curly hair, was waiting in the doorway. She appeared to be in her late twenties or early thirties.

'Hello, Miss Bergman, I'm Jane Marchant.' She smiled with real warmth, and, drawing Loris into a large panelled hall with a beautiful old staircase running up the centre, exclaimed, 'What absolutely dreadful weather! Let me take your wet things.'

Hanging Loris's raingear and her shoulder bag on the hall stand, she added cheerfully, 'Dinner's almost ready, but before you sit down to eat suppose I just quickly show you over the house? That way you can get some first impressions.'

Though the signs of neglect were only too obvious, Fenny Manor was both charming and spacious, a house of character, with thick walls and mullioned windows.

By the time the brief tour was completed and they had ended up in a big, homely kitchen, with oak settles and a flagged floor, Loris knew it was just the kind of place she'd love to work in.

Standing in front of the glowing stove, surveying the white plaster walls and black-beamed ceiling, she said as much.

'I'm pleased you like it.' Jane Marchant smiled her relief. 'It would have been a pity if you'd hated the sight of it, after being brave enough to turn out on such a miserable night.'

Returning her smile, Loris said, 'Door to door hardly counts as being brave. It's the taxi driver having to wait in the cold I feel sorry for.'

'Well, there's no need for the poor man to sit outside in the cab. I'll pull on my coat and go and ask him to come in.'

Hurrying to the door, she paused to say, 'By the way, that archway leads to the dining-room, if you'd like to go through...'

The dining-room was the only room Loris hadn't yet seen, but, deciding to wait for her hostess to return, she stayed where she was, wondering idly if there was a Mr Marchant.

There had seemed to be no one else at home, but Jane Marchant had said have dinner with *us* and, in the only bedroom that was furnished, Loris had noticed a man's hairbrush and a neatly-coiled tie.

What she hadn't noticed, and it only now struck her as strange, was any real sign of *feminine* occupation. Jane Marchant must be one of those tidy women who put everything away...

Bringing her mind back to practicalities, she turned her attention to the kitchen. The stove was standing in what had once been a huge fireplace—judging by the rough outline on the plaster—and set in the wall close by were two small oak doors to what, she guessed, was an old salt cupboard.

If the fireplace could be opened up again…

There had been no sound, but, suddenly convinced that someone was watching her, she swung round.

Standing silently in the archway, casually dressed in corduroy trousers and a black polo-necked sweater, was Jonathan Drummond.

As, hardly believing her eyes, she gaped at him, he said easily, 'I was wondering what was keeping you.'

'What on earth are *you* doing here?' she croaked.

'I live here. Or at least I will when everything has been sorted out.'

Advancing on her, he put a light hand at her waist, and urged, 'Do come through. Otherwise the meal will be past its best.'

Stunned and speechless, she allowed herself to be shepherded into a candle-lit dining room and seated at a long refectory table.

Watching her host—presuming he *was* her host—start to open a bottle of white wine, Loris realised with a strange sinking feeling that Jane Marchant must be the woman he wanted to marry.

She had introduced herself as *Mrs* Marchant, and when talking about his plans Jonathan had said the woman he was hoping to marry was involved with someone else at the moment.

And when she'd asked what he was doing here, he'd answered, 'I live here. Or at least I will when *everything has been sorted out*…'

So were they just waiting for Jane Marchant's divorce to come through before they officially moved in together? She had said, '*We've only recently bought Fenny Manor*…'

It was clear that on his salary Jonathan could never have

afforded to buy a place like this, so if they *were* partners *she* must be the one with money.

But after all his taunts about marrying for money, unless he was the world's biggest hypocrite, she couldn't imagine him getting married for *that* reason. He must love Jane Marchant...

Though if he did, and was so close to marrying the woman of his dreams, why had he taken *her* to bed?

The answer had to be that he was a red-blooded man who had seen the opportunity and seized it.

Much as Mark had with Pamela.

A one-night stand, with no feelings on either side.

Yet there had been something tender and caring about Jonathan's lovemaking. Something that had seemed to make the whole thing special.

Or was it simply her own response that had made her think so? Perhaps all *he'd* done was pretend he was making love to the woman he loved...

It shouldn't matter. But somehow it did.

As though following her thoughts, he asked, 'So what do you think of Jane?'

Loris swallowed. 'I like her very much.' Then, driven by the need to know for sure, she asked huskily, 'I suppose you *love* her?'

'Yes,' he answered simply.

Staring down at the white damask tablecloth, she wondered why, when she loved Mark and was about to marry him, the knowledge that Jonathan loved another woman was so bitter.

But *did* she love Mark? Wasn't it more that, she having decided she wanted a husband and a family, he'd been the only man to attract her? *Until Jonathan...*

No, she mustn't think like that. It was much too late. After wearing Mark's ring for three months, and with all their wedding plans made, there was no way she could change her mind now.

In any case, the whole thing was probably nothing more than pre-wedding nerves. Once they were married, she would know she'd done the right thing.

She was consoling herself with that thought when a little demon of doubt reared its ugly head to ask, but what if, when it was too late, she knew she'd done the *wrong* thing…?

'I hope you like Spanish food?' Jonathan's voice made her look up with a start.

Endeavouring to pull herself together, she answered, 'Yes, I do.'

Having filled first her glass and then his own with Chablis, he lifted the lid from a skillet keeping warm on a hotplate.

Watching as he began to serve the steaming rice dish, she became aware for the first time that the table was set for only two people. Puzzled, she asked, 'Isn't Mrs Marchant eating with us?'

The candle flame picking up a little glint in his eye, he answered, 'Jane doesn't like Paella.'

With a sudden realisation of how long her hostess had been gone, and remembering the state of the bridge, Loris asked urgently, 'Do you think she's all right?'

'I'm sure she is.' He appeared calm, unconcerned.

Shaking her head, Loris said, 'You don't understand—she went out to speak to the taxi driver. Surely she should have been back by now?'

'She won't be coming back.'

'What do you mean, she won't be coming back?'

'I mean she's going home.'

'Going home?' Loris echoed blankly. 'Doesn't she live here?'

'No, she lives over at Harefield.'

'Oh, but—'

'Please make a start on your meal before it gets cold,' he broke in firmly, 'and after we've eaten I'll be happy to tell you anything you want to know.'

Seeing by his face that she was going to get nowhere until she'd complied, Loris picked up her fork.

When their plates were empty, and she'd refused a piece of *torta*, he poured coffee for them both and suggested, 'Why don't we drink our coffee in front of the living-room fire?'

He pulled back her chair and ushered her into the adjoining room, which had oak-panelled walls and an arched door through to the hall.

It looked cosy and intimate, with a single standard lamp casting a pool of light and a log fire blazing cheerfully in a wide stone hearth.

In front of the fireplace was a thick, white sheepskin rug, and in a semicircle around it a comfortable-looking three-piece suite and an oval coffee table.

When Jane Marchant had briefly shown it to her Loris had thought it a most attractive room, and a second look served to confirm that conclusion.

'Let me take your jacket; it's warm in here.' Before she could demur, Jonathan had slipped her bilberry-coloured jacket from her shoulders and hung it over a chair.

Taking a deep breath, she began, 'Now perhaps you'll tell me—'

'Why don't you make yourself comfortable first?' he broke in smoothly, indicating the couch with a long, well-shaped hand.

Biting her lip, she reminded herself that, for the moment at least, he was calling the tune. Determined to keep as much space as possible between them, however, she avoided the couch and took a seat in the nearest armchair.

Smiling at her choice, he sat down on one of the wide arms of the chair and cocked an eyebrow at her expectantly.

All her awareness focused on the man by her side, Loris took a nervous gulp of her coffee. Then, trying to hide how disturbing it was to have him so close, she said as calmly as possible, 'Would you mind telling me why Mrs Marchant thought it necessary to mislead me?'

'I asked her to,' he admitted unrepentantly. 'I told her exactly what I wanted her to say… Though as it happens she had seen and admired some of your work, so that bit at least was true.'

'It must be the only bit that was.'

He sighed. 'She disliked having to mislead you, and only did it to please me.'

'I fail to see why it was necessary,' Loris said stiffly.

'Would you have come if *I'd* asked you to? Of course you wouldn't. The way things are at the moment you'd have run a mile first.'

'If you were so sure of that, I don't know what you hoped to gain by bringing me here under false pretences.'

His eyes on her face, he asked, 'Do you like the house?'

'Yes,' she admitted.

'Wouldn't you like to work on it?'

Of course she would—if he had no connection with it. As it was… 'No, I wouldn't,' she said flatly.

He raised a fair brow. 'Why not?'

'*Why not?* You must be joking! Mark and I are getting married in a week.'

'You told me you intended to keep working at least until June.'

'I do. But not for you. So I'm afraid you've wasted your time, and mine.' Feeling suffocated by his nearness, she struggled to her feet.

'Going somewhere?'

'Home,' she said succinctly.

'How are you planning to get there?'

'Just in case you've forgotten, I have a taxi waiting for me.'

Above the black polo-neck his hair looked bleached of colour, and his heavy-lidded eyes gleamed green as a cat's. 'I think not.'

Loris glanced at him sharply, then in response to his quiet air of certainty she hurried over to the window and, parting the curtains, peered out.

The living-room was at the front of the house, overlooking the river and the cobbled area where the taxi had drawn up to wait.

Through the pouring rain she could see the taxi was no longer there.

Turning on him, she demanded angrily, 'What did you do? Pay him off and tell him to go?'

'Not exactly.' He rose to face her. 'I suggested to Jane that she told him there was no need to wait, as you'd decided to stay the night, and then used the cab to get home herself.'

Her heart starting to thud against her ribs, Loris said, 'She must be very trusting if she was prepared to go off and leave another woman here...'

'She trusts me implicitly,' he assured her, straight-faced.

'I fail to see why she should, when she knows perfectly well that I had no intention of staying the night.'

'*Had?* Does that mean you've changed your mind?'

Gritting her teeth, she said, 'No, it *doesn't* mean I've changed my mind. So perhaps you'll be good enough to call me another taxi.'

'I'm afraid I left my mobile at the office, and the phone here isn't connected yet,' he said smoothly.

'You're lying. I rang Fenny Manor late this afternoon and spoke to Mrs Marchant.'

'I can assure you she was at Harefield then. I was with

her when she left the message, and also when you phoned back later.'

Thoroughly agitated now, Loris said, 'Well, as you're responsible for me being stranded here, I must ask you to drive me at least as far as the nearest phone box.'

'I'm afraid I have no transport, and even if I had it wouldn't be safe to drive over the bridge.'

'If you have no transport, how did you both get back from Harefield?'

'We came by taxi. After going through some deepish water on my way from London my car was playing up so, rather than chance getting stuck, I left it at Jane's to be looked at.'

He seemed to have an answer for everything, though she was convinced it was all just a clever fabrication.

Wondering what kind of game he was playing, what his intentions were, she fought down a feeling bordering on panic and announced firmly, 'Then I'll walk to the village and phone from there.'

'The way the water's still rising you'd have a job to make it on foot... And, apart from that, it must be getting a bit risky to cross the bridge.'

Shuddering at the memory, she nevertheless said, 'Well, I'll have to chance it. Anything's better than being trapped here.'

He smiled crookedly. 'Death before dishonour? How very melodramatic.'

'It's nothing to joke about,' she told him vexedly. 'Mrs Marchant may trust you now, but what would she say if she knew what happened on Saturday night?'

'I'm sure she wouldn't mind. Jane's extremely broad-minded.'

'Well, *Mark* isn't, and if he discovered I'd spent the night here alone with you—'

'Oh, we won't be alone. Elizabeth is here.'

'Elizabeth? Who's Elizabeth?'

Stooping to throw another log on the fire, he answered, 'Our resident ghost. A friendly one, so they tell me. Though I haven't encountered her personally.'

'*Will* you be serious for once? As I've absolutely no intention of working for you, and we're both about to get married...'

He gave her a quick sidelong glance from between thick gold-tipped lashes. His expression held a hint of amusement.

'You *are* aren't you?' she demanded.

'Hopefully.'

'Then what's the *point* of all this?'

Looking serious now, he said, 'I thought while we were both still single it would be nice to spend another night together.'

'*Nice!*' she choked. 'You must be out of your mind!'

'I'm aware that in the morning you had some second thoughts, but on the whole you seemed to enjoy it enough to be willing to repeat the experience.'

'You know what?' she said shakily. 'When you're on the point of marrying someone else, that's the most immoral suggestion I ever heard!'

He looked pained.

'I don't know how you had the nerve to criticise Mark,' she went on, two bright spots of angry colour appearing in her cheeks. 'Compared to you, he's practically a saint!'

Jonathan smiled derisively. 'He's very far from being a saint. Believe me, any criticism I made of Longton was quite justified. He's a womaniser and a bully. Look at the way he treated you.'

Taking her right hand, where the cuff of her cream silk blouse failed to hide a slight red mark, he gently touched his lips to the inside of her wrist.

It was the sort of thing Mark would never have dreamt

of doing, and, oddly shaken by the tenderness of the gesture, she jerked her wrist free.

'That was as much *your* fault as Mark's. If you hadn't gone out of your way to make trouble—'

'Now, is that a nice thing to say?' he complained.

'It may not be nice, but it's a fact. And one of these days, if you go on like this, you're going to end up in serious bother. Each time you've come up against Mark you've deliberately provoked him, and if I'd admitted it was *you* who told me the story about the mistress and the baby—'

'You didn't?'

'No, I didn't. In fact I convinced him it wasn't you. Otherwise you'd have had no job left by now.'

Finding it a relief to let off steam, she continued to berate him. 'You just don't seem to care; you were even late for the meeting, and in your position...'

Her voice tailed off as something struck her. 'You said you were at Harefield with Mrs Marchant when she left the message on my answering machine...?'

'That's right.' An unholy gleam in his eye told her he was following her train of thought.

'The message was timed at three-fifty. You should have still been at the office—so why weren't you?'

'I'll give you one guess.'

She half shook her head, unwilling to believe it.

When he said nothing, merely waited, she stammered, 'Y-you don't mean Mark...?'

'Fired me?'

'Did he?'

'He tried. As soon as I walked into the meeting he cursed me roundly and told me to get out.'

Concerned, despite herself, she asked, 'Couldn't William Grant help?'

'I didn't want him to. It suited me to go.'

Of course… Wasn't he planning to marry someone with money?

Wearily, she asked, 'So this plan to lure me down here and force me to stay the night, was it done simply for revenge?'

'What do you think?'

'I think you're utterly despicable.'

'That's a pity, because I think you're quite enchanting.'

Turning her back on him, she headed for the door.

For the second time that day he was there before her, his back to the panels.

'Please get out of my way,' she said curtly. 'I want to go.'

When he made no move, she insisted, 'I mean it. I'm not joking.'

'Neither am I, when I tell you I have no intention of letting you leave here at least until morning… And possibly not then.'

Her heart starting to throw itself against her ribs, she protested, 'You can't keep me here.'

'I rather think I can,' he corrected mildly.

'*Please*, Jonathan,' she begged.

'I intend to,' he assured her with a little smile. 'In fact I can promise you *delight*…'

'No!' Heat running through her, she whispered, 'I don't want to make love with you, and if you try to force me I'll never forgive you. Never!'

'I've no intention of trying to force you.'

Her relief was short-lived as he added, 'I'll find ways of pleasuring you that will make you more than willing to come to bed with me…'

Every nerve in her body tightened and, to her horror, she felt the stirrings of desire. Scared to death now, not so much of him as of her own reactions, she moistened her dry lips.

'You're starting to want me already, without me even touching you,' he taunted.

'No!'

'Don't lie to me, Loris, I can see it in your face, in the way your body is already responding to the mere thought.'

She had never in her wildest dreams imagined herself in this kind of predicament. For more than three months she had *tried* to respond to Mark's caresses, his passionate kisses, and not been as moved as this, so how could Jonathan affect her so strongly with just a look and a few words?

Aware that her nipples were growing firm, and terrified that he'd see the evidence of her arousal though the thin silk of her blouse, she crossed her arms over her chest.

The betraying gesture made him laugh softly.

Turning away abruptly, she went to stand by the fire. If she couldn't prevent herself weakening, she must find some way to hide it.

When Jonathan said he wouldn't try to force her, she believed him. If she could only say *no* and mean it, he wouldn't touch her.

But, as though he held the key to her newly awakened sexuality, her body was only too responsive, so it was all down to will-power.

CHAPTER EIGHT

WELL, she had never been short of that, Loris told herself hardily, then jumped a mile as Jonathan came to stand close behind her.

Moving aside the swathe of long dark hair, he touched his lips to the soft skin of her nape, making her shiver.

'Don't,' she said raggedly. 'I don't want you to touch me.'

'My sweet little liar...' He nibbled at the sensitive juncture where the neck and shoulder met. 'You *do* want me to touch you.'

He slid his hands over her ribcage and let them rest so that his thumbs just brushed the undersides of her breasts. She could feel their warmth through the fine crêpe de Chine of her blouse.

Standing irresolute, she wondered frantically what would be her best means of defence. Would it be to turn and fight, or try to ignore what he was doing to her?

Deciding on passive resistance, she feigned indifference while his mouth travelled slowly up the side of her neck, biting and teasing, sending little *frissons* of excitement running through her.

She was so busy trying to resist the delicious torment of his tongue-tip exploring the warm hollow behind her ear that she was scarcely aware of his fingers deftly undoing the buttons of her blouse.

Not until his hands were cupping breasts protected only by a dainty scrap of satin and lace did she fully appreciate her danger.

And then it was almost too late.

His thumbs were rubbing lightly across her nipples, arousing a suffocating excitement when, his lips brushing her ear, he whispered, 'I know quite well you're not indifferent. I can feel your heart pounding, and your breath coming faster.'

'That's revulsion,' she said thickly.

He laughed. 'I've always liked a woman to have a touch of fighting spirit.'

'If you don't take your hands off me this minute, I'll show you more than a *touch* of fighting spirit.'

'Be careful,' he warned, 'there's nothing that inflames a man's passion more than a struggle.'

Guessing he'd only said that to make her stand submissively, she pulled herself free and swung round, her hand raised to slap his face.

She gave a little gasp as his fingers closed around her wrist.

His grip loosened immediately. 'Forgive me, I forgot about the bruise.'

Then, holding her hand lightly, he offered his cheek. 'Feel free to go ahead and slap me if it will make you feel any better.'

The mocking smile that accompanied his offer was like a match to a powder keg.

Smiling back with saccharine sweetness, she said, 'I'm sure it will,' and, swinging her left hand, gave him a slap across the face that cracked like a pistol shot and jerked his head sideways.

For an instant they both froze. Then as he lifted his hand she flinched away, wishing desperately that she'd controlled the flare of temper.

Seeing that involuntary movement, he said quickly, reassuringly, 'It's all right.' Then, gingerly feeling his cheek, 'I'm only assessing the damage.'

Shaken to the core, because she was anything but a violent person, she said, 'I'm sorry. I shouldn't have done that.'

'I asked for it,' he admitted ruefully. 'It just came as something of a surprise…'

Perhaps he'd presumed she wouldn't have the nerve, Loris thought as she pulled her blouse together and began to fasten the buttons with unsteady fingers.

As though he'd walked into her mind and read her thoughts, with wry self-mockery he explained, 'If you'd used your right hand I would have felt the muscles tense and seen it coming. I just hadn't allowed for the fact that you might be ambidextrous.'

His attitude was amused, in no way menacing, and she started to breathe more freely. Though her body still clamoured for his touch, the moment of danger seemed to have passed.

She had won.

Tucking her blouse back into her skirt, she said as lightly as possible, 'Well, now you know I'm not a woman to be trifled with, perhaps you'll allow me to get my coat and leave.'

Smiling grimly, he said, 'My dear Loris, you've only won a preliminary skirmish, not the war.'

Before she could react to the threat in his voice, she found herself lying flat on her back on the sheepskin rug.

He had gone down with her, his arms breaking her fall. Even so, for a second or two she was shocked into stillness. Then she began to struggle furiously.

Gently, he pinned her arms above her head with one hand and used the weight of his body to hold her there.

She continued to writhe and struggle futilely, until, realising that he'd spoken the truth when he'd said, 'There's nothing that inflames a man's passion more than a struggle' she abruptly froze.

With a crooked smile, he said, 'Yes,' and watched as she

blushed hotly. 'But if, in the next five minutes, I can't make you admit you want me, then I promise I won't touch you.'

His free hand cupping her chin, so she couldn't turn her face away, he bent his head and kissed her lightly.

She kept her teeth clenched, and after a second or two his lips began to wander over her cheeks, her temples, her closed eyelids, bestowing soft, butterfly kisses.

When they returned to resume their teasing, she was forced to redouble her efforts to keep her mouth closed against him.

If his kisses had been hard and grinding she would have found it easier to fight, but these coaxing, beguiling little caresses that promised such delight made her *want* to open her mouth to him.

She shuddered as his tongue-tip traced the outline of her lips and slipped between them to tease the sensitive inner skin, but somehow she held on.

Slowly and carefully, for the second time that night, he undid the buttons of her blouse, and opening it, nuzzled his face against the swell of her breasts.

'Don't, please don't...' The words ended in a gasp, as through the thin scrap of ivory satin she felt the damp warmth of his breath.

A moment later he had released the front fastening of her bra and pushed aside the cups, giving him free access to her beautifully shaped breasts and dusky pink nipples.

As he teased them with mouth and fingers, causing needle-sharp sensations, she moaned a little, the exquisite pleasure almost too much to bear.

While his mouth continued its torment, his hand moved down to slip off her shoes, before returning to travel up over her nylon-clad calf and knee to find the band of bare skin above the lacy top of her stocking. It paused there for an instant before moving further to discover the dainty satin briefs.

As she held her breath, his fingertips followed the high-cut leg of her briefs up to her hip and back again. There they paused to softly stroke the silky skin of her inner thigh.

Her whole body was on fire now, alive with wanting. Nothing else existed but this man and what he was doing to her. There was no past, no future, only the here and now. and an overwhelming need.

But, instead of going on to fulfil that need, the hand was withdrawn.

Suddenly she found she was free, and Jonathan was standing looking down at her. As she lifted a dazed face he took both her hands and helped her to her feet.

Her eyes wide and unfocused, she staggered a little. Standing aloof, he caught her shoulders and steadied her.

'Jonathan, I...' Swaying towards him, she put her arms around his neck and pressed her body against his in a wordless plea.

Refusing to hold her, he insisted, 'I'd like to hear you say it.'

Thickly, she said, 'I want you to make love to me.'

'Well, first we'll have this off.' He removed the engagement ring she was wearing and tossed it carelessly onto the wide mantelshelf.

Then, refusing to hurry, making her wait, he began to undress her. When her skirt, blouse, half-slip and bra were in a pile on the floor, and she was standing in her stockings and briefs, he slipped his hands inside her briefs to cup her buttocks, before bending his head to tease her eager nipples with his tongue once more.

'Please...' she whispered, in an agony of suspense.

Straightening, he slipped off his shoes and socks, pulled his sweater over his head and tossed it aside, before taking her hands and guiding them to the belt on his trousers.

She had never undressed a man before and, eagerness making her clumsy, she had a struggle to undo the buckle.

When it was finally unfastened, she fumbled with shaking fingers to unclip the waist.

Taking pity on her, he did the rest for her, stepping out of the trousers and sliding his dark silk shorts over lean hips.

With shoulders much broader than she'd first imagined, his body was graceful and symmetrical. He carried not an ounce of spare flesh and had the toned fitness of an athlete, the muscles rippling beneath skin that was smooth and tanned and healthy.

As she stared at him, her throat dry, he ordered softly, 'Let me look at you.'

Obediently she pushed the briefs down and stepped out of them, then, one hand on his shoulder to steady herself, stripped off first one stocking and then the other.

When she was completely naked she stood and let him look his fill, feeling no embarrassment, only a sense of gladness that what he saw so obviously pleased him.

'You're *beautiful*,' he murmured, almost reverently.

'So are you,' she said huskily.

Taking her hands, he drew her to him, naked flesh to naked flesh, her head on his shoulder.

All urgency gone, for a moment she closed her eyes, content to just let him hold her. The warmth and the clean male smell of him were precious and *familiar*. It was like coming home after a long time in the wilderness.

Putting a hand beneath her chin, he turned her face up to his and kissed her softly.

It was the barest brushing of lips, but it felt like a commitment, and she knew without a doubt that she loved this man. Had loved him since the moment she'd first set eyes on him.

It was *right, inevitable, ordained*, even, that they should be lovers.

Drawing back a little, she smiled at him and touched his

cheek wonderingly. Then, with a single fingertip, she traced
first the cleft in his chin, and then his mouth—a mouth that,
with its combination of cool asceticism and warm sensu-
ality, always sent little quivers of excitement running
through her.

He took her hand and kissed the finger, then, putting the
tip in his mouth, sucked it.

Her stomach clenched, and abruptly the urgency was
back.

Reading that urgency, he reached to switch off the standard lamp, then, in the firelight's glow, drew her to him
and kissed her again, this time with passion and an urgency
of his own.

Opening her mouth to him, she put her arms around his
neck, and when he gently eased her down onto the thick
sheepskin rug she pulled him down with her.

Loris surfaced slowly, her whole being steeped in happiness
and a deep contentment. Her mood was languorous, her
body relaxed and well satisfied, sleek as a cat's.

For a while she lay, still half-asleep, savouring this feeling of bliss, remembering the previous night and Jonathan's
lovemaking. How he had ravished her—in the best meaning
of the word—the heights he had carried her to, the way his
promise of delight had been more than fulfilled.

She recalled the feel of the thick sheepskin rug beneath
her, the warmth of the fire on her bare flesh, the way the
leaping flames had gilded his face and hair and turned the
body poised above her into a golden-limbed Apollo.

Afterwards they had lain contented in each other's arms
until the fire had dwindled into glowing ashes and the air
had grown cool.

Unwilling to destroy that perfect aftermath, Loris would
have stayed there until morning if, feeling her slight shiver,

Jonathan hadn't gathered her up in his arms and carried her upstairs.

There, desire stirring once more, lighting up the darkness, they had made love until, sated, they had fallen asleep, her head on his chest, her body half supported by his.

Now she became aware that she was alone in the big bed, and watery sunlight was casting the shadows of the leaded windowpanes onto the white walls.

It was a new day.

With that realisation her brain kicked into action, and within seconds the icy wind of reality had shrivelled her happiness and blown it all away like so many dead leaves.

She might love Jonathan—and despite his faults she *did* love him, with all her heart and soul—but he wasn't hers to love. He belonged to another woman. He *loved* another woman.

Last night's determined seduction had meant nothing except that he'd *wanted* her. On his part it had been a purely physical thing, just a stolen night of passion that he should never have suggested. It had been utterly wrong of him.

She, in her turn, had been stupidly weak and wicked to agree to it. She had behaved very badly, not only as far as Mark was concerned, but Jane Marchant too.

What in heaven's name had she been thinking of?

In truth she hadn't been thinking at all. Only *feeling*. And now it was too late. The damage was done.

At least in *her* case.

Jonathan might be able to go on as if nothing had happened, but she couldn't. Last night had irrevocably altered things. How could she go ahead and marry Mark knowing full well she didn't love him?

The answer was, she couldn't.

But with all the wedding plans made how could she bring herself to tell him that she'd changed her mind? That it was all over? He was bound to take it badly, and she'd never wanted to hurt him.

Feeling bitterly ashamed, and guilty at the way she'd treated him, she stifled a groan. She'd always thought of herself as having reasonable morals, but now her actions had lowered her in her own eyes.

She had behaved like a wanton.

All at once, as though leaving Fenny Manor would enable her to leave some of the guilt behind her, she couldn't wait to get away.

There was still no sign of Jonathan, and the house felt quiet and somehow empty. A glance at her watch showed it was after twelve.

As she swung her feet to the floor she noticed two things: her clothes and shoes had been gathered up and placed neatly on a chair, and on the bedside table there was a cup of cold coffee with a folded piece of paper propped against it.

Opening the note with hands that were suddenly unsteady, she read it.

As time is getting on and we've a busy day ahead, I've decided to fetch the car. I wanted very much to kiss you before I left, but it seemed a shame to chance waking you. Love, J.

Love, J...

Her breath caught in her throat, and just for an instant a wild hope made her heart soar.

Then common sense brought her down to earth with a bump. It was no doubt just a casual, meaningless end to a note or letter, rather than a declaration of his feelings.

Of course he didn't love her. He'd already said he loved Jane Marchant.

As far as *he* was concerned last night had been simply an enjoyable episode, a last fling without any *involvement*.

If he knew how she felt he'd no doubt be uncomfortable, embarrassed by the unforeseen and unwanted complication.

It seemed she'd made a fool of herself all the way round. If he discovered the true state of affairs, what little was left of her self-respect would be trampled into the mud.

The only way she could keep any pride at all was to let him believe that last night had been no more to her than it had been to him.

If she *could*.

He'd written, '*we've* a busy day ahead', but if she spent the day with him she might be unable to hide how she felt... Which meant she must go now, at once, before he returned. Her secret would only be safe if she never had to see him again.

She had no idea how he would get to Harefield, or how long it would take him, but, judging by the cold coffee, he'd already been gone for some time.

He might be back at any minute.

Struggling out of bed, she made her way across to the *en suite* bathroom, where the scent of shower gel still hung in the air and drops of water clung to the frosted glass of the shower stall.

On a shelf, as though waiting for her, there was a Cellophane-wrapped toothbrush and a new tube of toothpaste.

She brushed her teeth and showered as quickly as possible, then, grimacing at having to wear yesterday's clothes, she ran a borrowed comb through her hair before hastening down the stairs.

She had pulled on her mac, thrust her rain hat into one of the pockets and gathered up her bag, when she remembered the ring.

It was on the mantelshelf where Jonathan had tossed it.

Dropping it into her bag, she hurried to the door once more, and as she pulled the door open exclaimed, 'Oh!'

An elderly woman, her face mirroring Loris's surprise, was standing on the doorstep, a key in her hand.

'Sorry, did I startle you?' she asked.

'I didn't know anyone else lived here,' Loris said, feeling foolish.

'I don't actually live here,' the woman explained. 'I just come in on a daily basis to take care of things. It's only five minutes' walk from my cottage, so it's nice and handy.'

Seeing her chance, Loris said, 'Well, if you're local, perhaps you can help me? I need to call a taxi, so can you tell me where the nearest phone box is?'

'Oh, if it's a taxi you're wanting, Jeff Middleton's your man. He owns the smallholding right at the end of the lane, but he runs a one-man taxi service on the side.'

'Thanks.' Throwing her a grateful smile, Loris hurried down the steps to the drive. It was still damp underfoot, but the sky was clear for the first time in days and overnight the level of the river had dropped.

In the daylight the bridge looked a great deal stronger and safer than it had done the previous night, and she crossed it without fear.

With its bare hedges and lack of trees there was no cover on the lane, and, her heart in her mouth in case Jonathan's car should appear, she started up it. Though the verges were muddy and waterlogged, the roadway itself was now clear of water and, alternately running and walking, she made good time.

She had just reached the end and identified the smallholding when she heard the sound of an approaching car.

Darting into the gravelled entrance, she hid behind a somewhat ramshackle hen-house while she watched Jonathan's white saloon drive past and turn down the lane.

'Is it eggs you're wanting?'

The voice made her jump. She turned to see a youngish, fresh-faced man wearing a thick navy sweater over a pair of scruffy trousers.

'No…no, thank you. I need to get into London, and I was hoping to hire a taxi.'

'When for?'

'Well, now.'

'Be with you in a minute. Just need to fasten up the goats. You can get in if you want.' He jerked a thumb at a beaten-up Cortina that stood in the drive.

She climbed in and slammed the door, thanking her lucky stars that she'd just made it in time.

Anxious as she was to get moving, it seemed an age before the man returned and, wiping his hands on a piece of oily rag, got behind the wheel.

'Second call out so far today,' he remarked as he turned the key in the ignition and the engine roared into life. 'Took the new owner of Fenny Manor over to Harefield this morning.'

With a grinding of gears and jerk or two they were off, their tyres crunching on the gravel. They were just about to pull out of the drive when, from nowhere it seemed, the white saloon appeared and drew up in front of them, blocking the exit.

Jonathan jumped out and came strolling over as Jeff Middleton rolled his window down.

'Hello again, Mr Drummond.'

'Afternoon, Jeff. I see you have my guest with you.'

'Just driving the young lady into London.'

'I'm going there myself, so I'll be happy to take her…'

'No, thanks, I'd rather go with Mr Middleton.'

Ignoring Loris's protest, Jonathan produced a small roll of notes which smoothly changed hands. 'Might as well save you a job.'

'Can't say I haven't got plenty to do,' Jeff agreed and, stuffing the notes into his pocket, climbed out of the car.

Jonathan came round to open Loris's door and, ignoring the angry look she gave him, helped her out.

His hand lightly holding her elbow, he escorted her over to his car and settled her in before slipping behind the wheel.

As always his touch set her pulses racing and made her breathless, and she had to struggle to hide how *conscious* she was of him.

They drove for a while without speaking, then he broke the silence to ask, 'So what made you decide to run away?'

'I wasn't running away, simply leaving. What did you expect me to do? Take up permanent residence?'

'Would that be such a bad thing?'

'I've never really fancied a *ménage à trois*,' she said coldly.

'If the thought of Elizabeth bothers you, I could always call in an exorcist.'

'It isn't the thought of *Elizabeth* that bothers me…'

'Well, I wasn't thinking of asking Longton to live with us.'

'Oh, you're quite *impossible*,' she snapped.

'If you keep on saying that I may well develop a complex,' he said plaintively.

'What I *could* do with you developing is the ability to stay out of my life,' she told him tartly, while her treacherous heart rejoiced just to be with him.

'Is that what you really want, now you won't be marrying Longton?'

She took a deep, steadying breath, and asked, 'What makes you think I won't be marrying him?'

Though she knew that her question had shaken him, Jonathan's voice was even as he observed, 'You're not wearing his ring.'

Feeling in her bag, she retrieved the ring and slipped it back on.

'You don't still intend to go through with the wedding?'

'Of course,' she lied.

His jaw tightened. 'I thought last night might have meant something to you? Might have made you change your mind?'

She tried to say something light, dismissive, but all at once tears pricked behind her eyes and she found herself unable to speak. Instead she shook her head.

'Very well, discounting last night,' he said almost roughly, 'Longton still isn't the man for you. You've just told me you don't fancy a *ménage à trois*, but that's what you're letting yourself in for. Though he wants you enough to marry you, he isn't prepared to give up his mistress—'

'That's not true. He swore he didn't have one and I believe him.'

There was a short silence, then, apparently realising he was getting nowhere, Jonathan changed tack. 'Where is Longton today?'

'He's away on business.'

'So you weren't planning to see him?'

'Not until tonight. If his plane isn't late he'll be at my flat for about six-thirty.'

Jonathan said no more, and they drove for the next few miles in silence. They were coming up to a pleasant-looking country pub and, pulling into the car park, he stopped the engine and suggested, 'You must be more than ready for a drink and something to eat?'

Her mind had been far too busy to let her think of food, but all of a sudden she felt thirsty. 'A cup of coffee wouldn't go amiss,' she agreed.

They made their way inside and, sitting by the window, ordered ham sandwiches and a pot of coffee.

Head bent, busy once more with her thoughts, Loris ate and drank abstractedly.

Studying her preoccupied face—the dark silky brows and lashes, the pure bone structure, the neat nose and lovely, passionate mouth—Jonathan thought she was the most exquisite thing he'd ever seen.

All at once becoming aware of his scrutiny, she glanced up.

'Penny for them?' he offered.

Without meaning to, she found herself admitting, 'I was thinking about Mrs Marchant.'

'Oh?'

'How long have you known her?'

'Quite a long time.'

'Then you knew her while you were still living in the States?'

'Yes. Jane and her husband came over to stay with me from time to time.'

Jonathan's remark made her wonder if he was responsible for the break-up of the other woman's marriage. If he was, it seemed to make things so much worse.

Her conscience bothering her, Loris asked, 'Wouldn't she be terribly upset if she found out about last night?'

'I very much doubt it. As I told you, she's extremely tolerant.' Seeing his companion frown, he observed, 'You don't look too happy?'

'I just can't understand any woman being that tolerant. Are you certain—?' She stopped speaking abruptly.

'Certain about *what*?' he asked.

'That she really loves you?'

'Oh, yes, I think she does.'

He sounded so laid back, so sure of himself, that for a moment Loris was silent, wondering about his values, how he regarded marriage.

She had thought, from some of the things he'd said, that

he had good old-fashioned principles. But suddenly she wasn't so certain. Suddenly she had doubts about what kind of man he really was.

Needing to know, she asked, 'What sort of marriage do you envisage?'

He raised a fair brow. 'In what way?'

'I mean do you intend to have one of those modern marriages where each partner goes their own way?'

'Good Lord, no! As far as I'm concerned that isn't a real marriage. I want total commitment on both sides, a loving and stable home in which to bring up our children.'

'So after you're married there'll be no more nights like last night?'

The devilish smile she had come to like so much danced in his eyes. 'I certainly hope so...'

Seeing the doubt on her face, he added, 'But I'd like the woman involved to be my wife.'

In one way it was the answer she had hoped for. It meant that she hadn't been wrong about him. But at the same time it was like a knife turning in her heart.

As she sat still and silent, trying to absorb the pain, he said casually, with a glance at his watch, 'I guess we'd better be moving.'

They had been late eating and it was mid-afternoon by the time they left the pub. In sharp contrast to the last time they had shared a pub meal the sky was a clear baby-blue and the day, though cold, was bright.

Their route into London was clogged by traffic, and while Jonathan concentrated on his driving Loris fell into a brown study.

By the time she surfaced they had reached the outskirts of town and were turning off the main road and into Bladen Place.

'This isn't where I live,' she said.

'No, I know it isn't.' He slid from behind the wheel and

came round to open her door. 'But I've stopped here to show you something.'

Bladen Place was a quiet cul-de-sac. Its two-storey houses, though not luxurious, looked well-built and well-maintained, with neatly kept front gardens.

As Loris got out, she noticed that at number 23, the house Jonathan had parked in front of, the bedroom curtains were still drawn.

Unlatching the gate, he led the way up the path and, taking a Yale key from his pocket, quietly opened the door.

The hallway was small, but very nicely furnished. Red-carpeted stairs led up to a long landing, with two closed doors.

As he drew her inside, she glanced at him, made uneasy by his manner. 'What—?'

He put a finger to her lips and said softly, seriously, 'For everyone's sake I was hoping to avoid this, but as I can't think of any other way to convince you… Go up the stairs and open the right-hand door.'

Seized by a sudden apprehension, she found herself pleading, 'Won't you come with me?'

Shaking his head, he said decidedly, 'My presence would only make things worse.'

As, not liking the situation at all, she hung back, he gave her a little push and whispered sternly, 'Go on, where's your fighting spirit?'

With the greatest reluctance, she began to climb the stairs. When she reached the landing, she glanced back.

The hall was empty and the front door was closed.

Her feet noiseless on the thick carpet, she approached the right-hand door. Gritting her teeth, she turned the knob and pushed the door open.

With a feeling of *déjà vu*, she saw two people in the big double bed. Propped up on pillows, they were lying in each other's arms. Mark's eyes were closed in sleep, but the woman was staring straight back at Loris.

The little scene brought back such bitter memories of Nigel and his paramour that Loris felt gall rise in her throat, and thought for a moment she was going to be sick.

But it was immediately obvious that this woman was no brazen slut. She was young, little more than a girl, dark-haired and dark-eyed, with a kind of fragile dignity and a pretty, gentle face.

Though she sat quite still, cradling Mark's dark head against her breast, her expression revealed a tumult of feeling. She looked uncomfortable and apprehensive, yet oddly determined...

The only thing she didn't look, Loris realised, was surprised. She had been *expecting* the door to open, *waiting* for it.

As though the tension had communicated itself to the sleeper, he stirred and grunted.

Pulling herself together, Loris quietly closed the door and, hurrying down the stairs, let herself out. As the latch clicked gently behind her, she heard a baby start to cry.

By the time she reached the pavement Jonathan had turned the car round and was waiting by the kerb. Desperate to leave that painful little scene behind her, she jumped in and fastened her seat belt.

Responding to that unspoken urgency Jonathan let out the clutch, and in a moment they were pulling out of the cul-de-sac and joining the main traffic stream.

With a glance at her white face, he queried, 'Sure you're all right?'

Unable to tell him that it was being reminded of Nigel that had upset her far more than seeing Mark in another woman's arms, she answered obliquely, 'I will be when I know the full facts.'

Jonathan looked doubtful. 'Are you sure you want to talk about it just yet?'

'Why not?' she asked bitterly. 'Seeing my fiancé in bed with another woman is starting to lose its sting. In fact it's getting to be a habit.'

'I'm sorry it was necessary to put you through that.' His regret sounded genuine. 'If you hadn't still been determined to marry Longton I would have spared you that shock.'

It *had* been a shock, but nowhere near the shock it might have been if she had continued to believe she was in love with Mark.

Taking a deep breath, she asked, 'How did you manage to engineer it?'

'It wasn't a set-up,' Jonathan denied quietly.

'It must have been. I could see from the girl's face that she was expecting me, and you had a key to the door.'

'Yes, she gave me a key, and, yes, she was expecting you about that time. But she didn't lure Longton there especially, if that's what you're thinking. Apparently he enjoys what he calls "a spot of afternoon delight", and makes a habit of going to his love-nest two or three times a week. For one thing, it's easier to cover his tracks in the daytime. All he needs to do is say he's out on business, and who's to know he's spent most of the time in bed with his mistress? Take today, for instance. You thought he was away on business. Well, he was. He simply caught an earlier flight back to give him a few hours free.'

'I still don't understand how you know all this. How you became involved. Why you went to all this trouble. Why it *matters* to you. It has to be something more than mere disapproval, or even enmity...'

'It matters to me because the girl who was with him is Linda Marchant, Jane's sister-in-law, and Jane cares about her.'

CHAPTER NINE

THAT simple fact explained everything—why Jonathan had seduced her after the St Valentine's party, why he'd kissed her in BLC's foyer, why he'd lured her down to Fenny Manor...

In short, it explained why he'd been so determined to prevent her marrying Mark. It was for the sake of the woman he loved.

It even explained why Jane Marchant had been so willing to help him...

Loris felt as though a giant fist had closed around her heart and was squeezing the life out of it.

'What did you think of Linda?' Jonathan's tense question broke into her thoughts.

'Does it matter what I thought of her?' she asked wearily.

'Yes. It matters to me.'

Sighing, she answered truthfully, 'I thought she looked young and sweet, and surprisingly innocent.'

Jonathan's expression relaxed a little. 'She's far from being a tart. She was just seventeen and a naïve schoolgirl when he first seduced her. She's only nineteen now, and a really nice person. It's a great pity she's so crazy about that lying—' He broke off abruptly.

After a moment he continued more mildly, 'Believe me, both she and Jane were sincerely sorry to do this to you. They only agreed to my plan because Linda was desperate to keep the father of her child and Jane wanted to help. I hope you'll be able to forgive all three of us.'

'I suppose I should be thanking you for saving me.' Picking up the irony in the words, he frowned.

When she said nothing further, he asked carefully, 'Have you decided what you're going to do?'

Unhesitatingly, she answered, 'I shall give Mark back his ring.' And without too many qualms.

There was no mistaking Jonathan's relief.

'When I left you to go upstairs on your own I wondered if he'd succeed in talking his way out of it... But you weren't in the house for more than a minute, so I presume he either didn't try to make excuses or you didn't stay to listen to them?'

'He didn't even see me. He was asleep.'

'That might save a great deal of trouble. Linda was worried to death about having to try and explain how you came to know enough to be there at just the right time, and also how you got in... Unless you intend to tell him everything when you give him back his ring?'

'No, I don't. I shall merely tell him that I *know* he lied to me. Then as far as I'm concerned the whole thing's over and done with. I just hope she manages to find some happiness with him. I know now I never could have.' In spite of all her efforts, her voice sounded forlorn.

Jonathan reached over and gave her hand a quick squeeze. 'You'll find your share of happiness, I promise.'

It seemed unlikely, to say the least, when the man she had fallen in love with had merely used her to help the woman *he* loved.

She took a deep, shuddering breath and began, 'Tell me something...'

When she paused, trying to think how best to phrase it, he gave her a sidelong glance and asked encouragingly, 'What would you like to know?'

'I was wondering if your coming over to England with Cosby's was just a coincidence, or did you *choose* to come?'

'It wasn't a coincidence.'

'So you came over purposely to stop me from marrying Mark?'

'You could say that.'

A little edge to her voice, she said, 'Well, your mission's succeeded.' Then, with concern, 'But in the process you've lost your job... Unless Cosby's would let you work for them in the States?'

'I'm sure they would. But, having just acquired Fenny Manor, I don't happen to want to go back to the States. In any case, I'm hoping to be married quite soon.'

'Of course.'

And, as Jane Marchant obviously had money, he was under no immediate pressure. Though she couldn't believe he was the sort of man who would be content to let a woman keep him for any length of time...

Slanting her a glance, he remarked, 'You don't sound too happy about it.'

'Why shouldn't I be?' she said desperately. 'But I was just thinking that when you've got a wife to support it might be as well to have an income. What if I can persuade Mark to give you back your London job?'

His voice suddenly cold as ice, Jonathan queried, 'And how would you do that?'

'Not the way *you're* thinking.'

'I'm glad about that. I should hate to have to break his neck after all. So how?'

'A spot of blackmail.'

Looking amused now, he said, 'I hadn't figured you as a blackmailer. But do go on, you intrigue me.'

'Well, I could save his pride by telling my father and all his posh friends that we've decided we just aren't compatible... Or I could threaten to tell them exactly *why* I'd decided to end the engagement.'

Jonathan laughed. 'Simple, but I dare say very effective.'

Reaching for her hand, he raised it to his lips and kissed

the palm. 'Thank you, my love, I'm grateful. However, it's not necessary. I've no intention of working for Longton.'

Shaken by the endearment, Loris bit her lip. If only she *was* his love…

Perhaps, subconsciously, she'd wanted that since the moment they'd met. It had been so short a time, a matter of days, yet his effect on her life had been powerful.

But so much of it had been for the good.

If she'd married Mark she would have ended up as bitter and disillusioned as her mother. Jonathan, albeit for his own ends, had saved her from that, and she should be grateful.

Rather than have a husband like Mark, it was better not to marry at all. Though it was sad when, for the first time, she felt a whole woman and longed for the warmth of a loving relationship.

But not just *any* relationship.

She knew now that Jonathan was all she'd ever wanted, a man she could have been happy with, and she envied Jane Marchant with a wrenching envy that felt as if it was tearing her apart.

But envy wasn't a pleasant emotion, she reminded herself, and Jane Marchant—after having one failed marriage—was entitled to a second chance of happiness, to a husband who loved her, and a family.

The very things she herself wanted.

But unless, some time in the future, another man came along that she could love—and in the light of what had happened so far that seemed extremely unlikely—her career would have to take the place of a husband and family.

For once, the thought of her career failed to cheer her.

The Friday-night traffic proved to be unduly heavy, and, roadworks causing a bottleneck on the route Jonathan had chosen, they found themselves crawling along in a stop-start queue for several miles.

Refusing to get stressed, he put on some relaxing music

and whistled quietly to it, while Loris, tired from the previous night's lack of sleep and a veritable turmoil of emotions, leaned her head against the padded headrest and closed her eyes.

She was just rousing when Jonathan's voice said cheerfully, 'Here we are at last.'

Refreshed, she opened her eyes to find they had reached the block of flats where she lived and were turning into the underground car park.

Wondering how he'd known exactly where to bring her, she informed him, 'I'm afraid you're not allowed down here. It's for residents only.'

Taking not the slightest bit of notice, he drove down the long steep ramp until he reached the barrier.

In her smuggest 'you should have listened to me' voice, she said, 'I'm afraid you'll have to back up now.'

Green eyes glinting, he asked, 'Oh, why's that?'

'Because you have to have a resident's swipe card to raise the barrier.'

'You mean like this?' Producing a blue and white plastic card from his pocket, he swiped it through, and obediently the barrier rose.

A moment later he was pulling into one of the numbered parking bays. Catching sight of her expression, he asked innocently, 'Isn't this allowed either?'

'Not unless you're a resident, and this happens to be your bay.'

'I am, and it is.'

'What?' she said, failing to understand.

'I said I *am* a resident, and this *is* my parking bay.'

'But this is where *I* live,' she objected stupidly. He put on a thunderstruck expression. 'Gosh! Does that mean we're actually neighbours?'

'I do wish you'd be serious,' she said, not for the first time.

'While we're living in the same building I'll be the soul of gravity,' he assured her, and, jumping out, came round to open her door.

As they crossed to the lifts she tried to make sense of it. 'How do you come to be living here?'

'Simple. One of the service flats became vacant and I took a short lease on it.'

Strange things *did* happen, but with all the accommodation available in London surely this was too much of a coincidence? However, seeing by the gleam in his eye that he was quite prepared to go on teasing her, she decided to let the matter drop, merely asking, 'Which floor do you live on?'

'The same as you.'

'In a minute you'll be telling me you have the next-door flat.'

'I'm afraid not,' he said regretfully. 'We're at opposite ends of the building.'

When the lift stopped at the seventh floor he followed her out and turned to walk with her.

'I thought you lived at the opposite end?'

'So I do,' he agreed, unperturbed.

On reaching her door, he waited while she fished in her bag for the key, then opened the door for her.

'Thank you.' As steadily as possible, she added, 'I suppose, unless we meet by chance, this is goodbye.' She held out her hand.

'How very formal,' he mocked gently. Ignoring the proffered hand, he tilted her chin and kissed her lips.

A lover's kiss, it was bestowed with a possessive ardour that knocked her off balance and made her feel giddy. It seemed to offer a commitment and ask for a response.

When finally he raised his head, she lifted heavy lids and gazed up at him. Her golden eyes looked dazed, the pupils large and black.

Putting an arm around her waist, he urged her inside and closed the door behind them, before following her through the tiny hall and into the living-room.

Trying hard to regain her equilibrium, she queried thickly, 'If you intended to come in, why did you kiss me goodbye?'

'Oh, I didn't kiss you *goodbye*. I just took the opportunity to kiss you.' Glancing at her from beneath long gold-tipped lashes, he confided, 'I enjoy kissing you.'

Feeling she ought to scold him, but unable to, she stayed silent.

Looking around the living-room, with its beige and cream colour scheme, he remarked casually, 'All these flats are alike. Quite pleasant, but impersonal and far from exciting.'

Vexed that, while she was still shaken to the core, he could sound so unmoved and prosaic, she asked tartly, 'Did you follow me in for the sole purpose of criticising the decor?'

'Certainly not. There are much more important things to be done...' Then, with a hint of satisfaction, 'You told me Longton was coming at six-thirty, so if he didn't get held up he should be arriving any minute...'

A sudden suspicion made her ask, 'You weren't thinking of being here when Mark comes?'

'Of course.'

Fearing trouble, she cried sharply, 'No, I want you to go now! I don't want you to be here.'

'I'll keep out of it and let you handle things, if that's what you want, but I've no intention of leaving you alone.'

Knowing he was thinking of the slight bruise on her wrist, she said, 'No, really, there's absolutely no need to stay.'

His face serious, he asked, 'Just suppose Longton lost

his head and decided to use a little force to get what he's always wanted?'

Shocked, she whispered, 'No, he wouldn't.'

'Can you be certain of that?'

Could she?

Seeing the doubt on her face, he said grimly, 'Well, I've absolutely no intention of chancing it.'

The peal of the doorbell cut through his words.

'Stay here,' she hissed at him and, closing the door between the living-room and the hall, went to answer it.

Wearing a dark, well-tailored business suit, Mark was waiting. Looking a little surprised when she didn't immediately invite him in, he bent to kiss her.

She turned her head sharply away, so that his lips just brushed her cheek.

He frowned. 'Something wrong?'

'Yes.' Pulling off her engagement ring, she handed it to him.

Surprised into taking it, he stood staring down at the sparkling half-hoop of diamonds, before demanding angrily, 'What's going on? Why have you given me back my ring?'

'Our engagement's over,' she told him flatly.

'Don't be a fool. We're getting married in a week's time.'

'We're not getting married at all. You can tell everyone that we realised just in time that we aren't compatible.'

'Aren't compatible? Of course we're compatible! I don't know what's brought this on...' Then, a shade guiltily, 'Unless it's my sacking Drummond...? Look, let's go in and talk about it...'

Her heart in her mouth, she stood her ground. 'There's nothing to talk about. Unless you'd like to tell me where you spent the afternoon?' Watching some of the colour leave his face, she said, 'No, I didn't think you would.'

'Don't be idiotic, Loris,' he blustered, 'you know perfectly well I've been away on business.'

'You might have been on business this morning, but this afternoon you were visiting your mistress.'

'Whoever told you that was lying—'

'It isn't a lie, and you know it.'

'Believe me—'

'It's no use, Mark I *know*.'

'I don't see how you can *know* something that isn't true—'

'But it *is* true. You were at 23 Bladen Place, which is a quiet little cul-de-sac off Bladen Road. While you were there, the bedroom curtains were closed—'

His heavy face turning brick-red, he burst out, 'How the hell could you know a thing like that, unless you were having me followed?'

When she failed to deny it, he seized her hand. 'All right, so I admit I was there. But you're the only woman who means anything to me. It was just sex, and once we're married—'

Freeing her hand, she said wearily, 'I've heard that before from you and I just don't believe it. You'd better go, Mark.'

'If only you'd be prepared to forgive and forget, and marry me, I promise—'

'No more promises.' Her own conscience far from clear, she went on, 'I'm prepared to forgive and forget, but I'm not prepared to marry you.'

'Look, I'm sorry I lied to you—'

'It's not just that. I've realised I made a bad mistake. I don't love you, and there's no way I can marry a man I don't love.'

Seeing by his face that he was apparently genuinely upset, she added, 'I'm sorry, Mark, I never meant to hurt you. But it really *is* all over between us.'

Hearing the finality in her voice, he thrust the ring into his pocket and turned to walk towards the lifts.

Thankful that it was over, Loris closed the door and, trembling in every limb, went back to the living-room and sank into a chair.

Turning away from the window, where he'd been standing looking over the lights of Chelsea towards the river, Jonathan asked quietly, 'Was it very traumatic?'

'It wouldn't have been as bad if I hadn't felt so conscience-stricken.'

'Compared to Longton, you've very little to feel conscience-stricken about.'

'I don't know how you can take things so lightly,' she said with some asperity. 'You know quite well that we're both as bad as Mark.'

'Though I agree that neither of us are *entirely* blameless, I really don't think we belong in that category,' he objected mildly. 'However, as it's getting on for seven, we must leave that discussion until some other time.'

Taking her hands, he drew her to her feet. 'You've got about half an hour to get dolled up and—'

'Why do I need to get dolled up?' she broke in. 'I'm not going anywhere.'

'We're going out to dinner.'

'Oh, no. I—'

'Do you want to sit in and mope?'

'No, of course not…'

'So it's dinner at La Ronde and then we'll be spending the night at—'

'Are you crazy?' she cried. 'I've no intention of spending another night with you!'

He sighed. 'That's a shame… And just when I was starting to think you're getting to like the idea of being seduced.'

'As you've already achieved what you set out to do,

there's no further need to seduce me,' she pointed out with betraying bitterness.

'I wasn't intending to,' he assured her easily. 'At least not tonight. Tonight will be the height of propriety. We shall have different rooms and be well-chaperoned. But as we haven't got a lot of time, I'll explain the whole thing later... Now, go and get ready, there's a good girl. Oh, and don't forget to pack your night things, a change of undies, and your prettiest suit or dress, just in case.'

'But I—'

'No more arguments now. All the arrangements are made.' Opening the bedroom door, he gave her a gentle push. 'Off you go.'

Feeling as dazed and buffeted as if she'd been gathered up and swept along by some whirlwind, she pulled the door to behind her and began to sort through her drawers and wardrobe.

Having packed her overnight bag, and laid out the clothes she intended to wear, she went into the bathroom and, stripping off, stepped under the shower, her thoughts in a turmoil.

His self-imposed task accomplished, she had expected Jonathan to walk quietly away. That he should have further plans had come as a complete surprise, and she wondered uneasily what he was up to.

But, in spite of all her misgivings, her heart was beating faster with excitement and her spirits had risen with a bound at the prospect of spending the evening in his company.

Dried and perfumed, her flawless skin and dark brows and lashes needing no make-up, she coiled her hair into a gleaming knot on top of her head before putting on a calf-length silk evening dress.

A simply-cut sheath that she'd seen in Harrods and

bought in a rare moment of extravagance, it was a mix of tawny colours that echoed the gold of her eyes.

With it was a plain bronze jacket that somehow added to the exotic effect. Dull gold shoes and a matching bag finished off the ensemble.

Ready, she hesitated, her misgivings as to whether what she was doing was *sane* returning in force. Wouldn't spending more time with him only make the inevitable parting worse?

Perhaps, both for Jane Marchant's sake, and her own, she should dig in her heels and refuse to be coerced?

But soon he would be going out of her life for ever, and this last chance to spend a few more bittersweet hours in his company was far too precious to waste.

Picking up her small case, she opened the door to the living-room. Profiled against the dark window, Jonathan was standing quite still, staring blindly at the carpet, obviously deep in thought.

He must have been back to his own flat, she realised, because he was freshly shaved and had changed into impeccable evening dress.

For a moment she watched him unobserved, drinking in the sight of him, his lithe figure, his handsome profile, his hair, darkened and still a little damp from the shower.

As though her silent scrutiny had disturbed his concentration, he glanced her way.

There was a look on his face that she had never seen before. A look of doubt, of uncertainty, as if he had suddenly lost confidence in himself and whatever it was he'd been planning.

Almost instantly that look was gone, replaced by his usual quiet assurance.

His eyes swept slowly over her from head to toe. 'Wow!' he said softly. 'You look absolutely stunning...'

Absurdly pleased by his approval, she felt herself blushing.

Watching the colour rise in her cheeks, he remarked, 'And no lipstick. Even better!'

'You don't like lipstick?'

'I prefer you without. It means I can kiss you.'

Before she could object, he was suiting the action to the words.

When he released her, she said weakly, 'You shouldn't kiss me. It's not fair to Mrs Marchant.'

'Will it stop you worrying if I tell you that Jane won't mind in the slightest?'

'No,' Loris said unhappily, 'she *ought* to mind. Pretending not to mind puts her in the same class as Linda. Is that what you want?'

'Heaven forbid!' Jonathan exclaimed piously, and, taking her case, hurried her to the door. 'If we don't get a move on we're going to be late.'

The evening traffic was heavy, as usual, and it was a few minutes before eight when they reached Mayfair and drew up outside the restaurant.

La Ronde was both modern and imposing, a single-storey circular building, with an overhanging roof and lots of slanting smoked-glass windows.

Having helped her out, Jonathan handed over his ignition keys to one of several attendants in evening dress who were parking the cars.

Loris saw he was accorded the same deference as the man who had preceded them driving a Rolls-Royce.

The whole place had an air of opulence that oozed money, and Loris wondered nervously if her companion realised what he was letting himself in for.

A hand at her waist, he escorted her up the steps and into the foyer where they were immediately greeted by a grey-haired man in immaculate evening dress.

'Good evening, Mr Drummond. The rest of your party have already arrived and are waiting in the bar.'

Looking entirely at ease, as if he belonged in these sumptuous surroundings, Jonathan said casually, 'Thanks, we'll go through.'

Wondering who 'the rest of the party' could be, Loris allowed herself to be ushered into the bar, where a few well-dressed people were seated, either on bar stools or at small glass-topped tables.

A hand beneath her elbow, Jonathan steered her towards one of the tables where a young couple were sitting chatting.

The woman who was seated with her back to them had fair curly hair, while the nice-looking man sitting opposite her was dark.

At their approach, the nice-looking man rose to his feet and gave them a friendly smile. At the same instant his companion turned her head.

The woman with him was Jane Marchant.

Loris caught her breath.

Knowing there was no way she could face an evening in Jane Marchant's company, she would have turned and run, but, as though reading her mind, Jonathan put his arm around her and, ignoring her beseeching glance, urged her forward.

Short of creating a scene, there was little she could do, and a moment later he was making the introductions.

'My sister Jane, you already know...'

Sister! Jane Marchant was Jonathan's sister! Loris tried hard not to blush as she recalled the conclusions she'd jumped to.

'Hello, again.' Jane Marchant, looking pretty in powder-blue, gave Loris a somewhat uncertain smile.

'And this is David Marchant, Jane's husband. David, I'd like you to meet Loris Bergman...'

Feeling as though she was in a dream, Loris said, 'How do you do?' and held out her hand, liking this tall, spare man on sight.

His fingers closed over hers in a firm grip. 'It's nice to meet you. I gather that my wife and brother-in-law have rather turned your life upside down.'

'You weren't supposed to say that!' Jane scolded.

Unabashed, he asked Loris, 'All the same, it's true, isn't it?'

'Quite true,' she agreed, and they smiled at each other like conspirators.

Watching the pair of them, her relief obvious, Jane said, 'I have to admit I owe you an abject apology, Miss Bergman.'

'Please, won't you call me Loris? And there's no need for any apologies. I just hope that things work out for your sister-in-law.'

'Thank you. That's very generous of you.'

Jonathan took Loris's hand and gave it a squeeze, just as the *maître d'* appeared to show them to their table.

The restaurant was spectacular: its tables, set with crystal glasses and fresh flowers, were by the windows, widely spaced, and arranged like the spokes of a wheel.

'Isn't this lovely?' Jane exclaimed. Then, turning to Loris, she added sincerely, 'I'm so pleased you decided to come. I did wonder if Jonathan would be able to persuade you.'

'At one point I thought even my abundant charm might not be enough to do the trick,' he said ironically.

'Charm, my foot,' Loris retorted, 'he simply bulldozed me.'

They all laughed, and, the ice well and truly broken, took their seats.

The evening proved to be a great success. Both Jane and her husband were warm and outgoing, and while they ate an excellent meal, and drank a glass of vintage champagne, the conversation flowed easily.

By tacit consent they kept the topics light and impersonal, and with Jane's gentle wit complementing Jonathan's dry sense of humour they laughed a lot.

But while Loris listened and smiled and contributed a word here and there, part of her mind was mulling over what she'd learnt.

During the drive to Paddleham that first night Jonathan had mentioned a married sister, and now Jane and he were together she could see the faint likeness she'd missed earlier.

If only she hadn't jumped to entirely the wrong conclusion it would have saved her a great deal of anguish...

Or if Jonathan had told her the simple truth.

It must have been quite plain that she believed Jane to be the woman he was hoping to marry and, though he'd been careful not to tell her any lies, he'd allowed—no, *encouraged*—her to go on believing it.

But why? He must have had a reason.

Sighing inwardly, Loris resolutely pushed away the unsolved puzzle and made an effort to join more fully in the conversation.

As soon as the dessert plates had been cleared away, Jane gathered up her evening bag and, smiling, said to Jonathan, 'I think it's high time we were on our way. Give you and Loris a chance to talk.'

Both men rose with her, and David pulled out her chair.

Surprised by the suddenness, Loris asked, 'Aren't you staying for coffee?'

Patting her still-flat stomach, Jane announced cheerfully, 'Since I've been pregnant I've gone off both coffee and tea...'

Putting an arm around her, David said, 'And, apart from that, as prospective parents we need our quota of sleep.'

'Thank you both for a lovely evening,' Jane added. Then, a shade hesitantly, 'Hope to see you in the morning. Bye, now.'

David smiled at Loris and clapped Jonathan on the shoulder before turning to follow his wife.

'Alone at last!' Jonathan said dramatically. Reaching across the table, he took Loris's hand, and, lifting it to his lips, dropped a kiss into the palm.

The romantic little gesture rocked her.

His eyes on her face, he said, 'I hope the evening hasn't been too much of a strain?'

'Not at all.' Her voice wasn't quite steady. 'I liked both your *sister* and her husband.'

'I'm pleased.'

'Why didn't you tell me she was your sister?'

'If you remember, I did.'

'I mean *before* this evening…'

A waiter brought coffee and the conversation stopped until he'd served them both and moved away.

Taking a deep breath, Loris went back to the attack. 'You must have realised that I thought she was the woman you wanted to marry?'

'Yes, I did,' he admitted.

'Then why did you let me go on thinking it?'

'I'll tell you later. In the meantime, you tell me what made you jump to that conclusion?'

'You'd mentioned previously that you had plans to marry, but that the woman in question was "involved with someone else". So when Jane introduced herself as Mrs Marchant, and you said you loved her and she loved you, it seemed logical that she was the one…'

When he said nothing, she added, 'But obviously it's some other woman you're hoping to marry?'

'That's right.'

He was giving her no help, but, needing to *know*, Loris pursued, 'And I think you said *soon*?'

'Very soon.'

'But there are still some problems?'

'One or two.'

'Presumably you're waiting for this other relationship she's involved in to come to an end?'

'That's over, thank the Lord. But I may have a job persuading her to marry a man that her family will undoubtedly object to and who's just been fired.'

'Will either of those things bother her?'

'Wouldn't they bother you?'

'Not if I wanted to marry the man.'

'Do you?'

'Do I what?'

'Want to marry me?'

After a moment, she asked huskily, 'Is this some kind of joke?'

'It's more in the nature of a proposal.'

'A proposal!'

'I admit it's not the tender, romantic kind you read about in novels. If there'd been a rose garden handy, and a spot of moonlight, I could have gone down on one knee and asked for your hand in the traditional way. But as it's February, and pitch-dark...'

'I wish you'd be serious,' she said faintly.

His green eyes glinted. 'I've never been more serious in my life'

'You can't mean *I'm*...'

'The woman I want to marry? The woman of my dreams? The very same.'

Hardly daring to hope, still unsure whether he might just be teasing her, she said, 'But it's barely a week since you set eyes on me.'

'It's rather longer than that,' he contradicted. 'I saw you

when I first came over to England nearly six weeks ago. You came into the offices one day. I gather you had a lunch date with Longton. I knew then I wanted to marry you, and that helping Linda was a secondary consideration. But planning takes time, and I couldn't afford to make any mistakes.

'Of course it helped things along enormously when you and Longton quarrelled during the party and he went off with Pamela Gresham. If that little plan hadn't succeeded I would have had to think of some other way to get close to you...'

'What do you mean, *"if that little plan hadn't succeeded"*? You couldn't possibly have influenced what Mark and Pamela Gresham did...'

Watching his face, she knew she'd been wrong. 'I don't see *how*...' she faltered to a halt.

'I have a confession to make. As a matter of fact there's no such person as Pamela Gresham. Her name is Pamela Bradley, and I hired her from an—er—escort agency.'

Half-amused, half-appalled, Loris shook her head in disbelief. 'You hired a *call-girl*! How could you *do* such a thing?'

'All's fair in love and war, darling. And if Longton had been halfway decent he wouldn't have acted the way he did. Don't look so appalled. You must see he didn't love you any more than you loved him.'

Loris raised an eyebrow at his arrogant statement. 'What makes you so sure I didn't love him?'

He replied confidently, 'You're not the kind of woman who would cheat on a man she loved. The fact that you spent the night with me proved you didn't love him. But I wanted you to realise that for yourself, and admit it. However, after one look at your face the next morning, I knew I was in for an uphill struggle. Later, when we talked in the pub, though you *said* you loved Longton I knew you were just fooling yourself, and I was hoping against hope that if there was a showdown you'd come back to London with me. But when you told him the truth about sleeping with me and he magnanimously ''forgave'' you, despite not really believing you, I was back to square one. That's why it was necessary to involve Jane. What she did, she did for *me* as much as for Linda.'

'You still haven't told me why you allowed me to go on believing that Jane was the woman you were hoping to marry.'

'I wanted to see if, believing that, you would still sleep with me. The very fact that you did told me a lot.'

'I don't understand,' Loris said, bewildered.

'Leaving Longton out of it, you didn't seem to be the kind of woman who would make love with another woman's man unless you couldn't help yourself.'

Watching the colour come into her cheeks, he said, 'I needed to be sure so I could complete the arrangements.'

'What arrangements?' she asked suspiciously.

'For our wedding. I'd already got a special licence, but there were still things to organise. That's why I went over to Harefield. Then again, you shook me rigid by trying to run away the minute my back was turned, and insisting you still intended to marry Longton. That's why I was forced to take you to Bladen Place instead of shopping for a wedding dress, as I'd hoped. And, speaking of wedding dresses, you haven't said *yes* yet...'

He sounded so confident, so sure of her answer, while all Loris could feel was dazed, incapable of coherent thought. He already had a special licence!

Looking at her quizzically, he added, 'I must warn you that if you don't say yes at once I shall have to take you in my arms and kiss you until you do.'

'You can't kiss me here, in front of everybody,' she protested thickly.

'Do you want to bet?' He rose to his feet.

'Yes.'

Still standing, he asked, 'Is that yes you want to bet, or yes you'll marry me?'

'Yes, I'll marry you.'

'Good.' Resuming his seat, he added with a twinkle, 'That means we'll be able to come here again.' Then, watching her expressive face, 'What's wrong? Don't you like the place?'

'Oh, yes...' A shade awkwardly, she added, 'But it's bound to be very expensive.'

'I see. Will not being rich bother you?'

'Why should it? I've never been rich.'

'Your parents may not have loaded you with money, but you come from a rich background.'

Something in his tone made her ask, 'Does *that* bother you?'

He smiled at her. 'Not any longer. Now let's get out of here. I'm dying to kiss you.'

CHAPTER TEN

LA RONDE'S organisation was super-efficient, and by the time Jonathan had paid the bill and they had got outside his car was waiting, one of the attendants holding open the door.

A generous tip changed hands, and within seconds they were drawing away and joining the busy traffic stream to head out of town.

Sitting still and silent, Loris struggled to get her thoughts and emotions into some kind of order. The fact that everything had miraculously come right and she was going to marry the man she loved had barely sunk in.

Stunned by the speed at which things had happened, and the sheer unexpectedness of Jonathan's proposal, she hadn't even had time to feel happy.

Remembering his quiet admission of what lengths he'd gone to to break up her engagement, she gave a little shiver that was part excitement and part unease. Such ruthless determination scared her a little...

They had left the suburbs behind them and were on a quiet country road, their headlights picking up bare hedgerows, when she surfaced to ask, 'Where are we going?'

'Down to Harefield Farm. We're staying the night with Jane and David. Then all the arrangements are made for us to be married in the village church at twelve o'clock.'

Casually, he added, 'Though it will be a very quiet wedding, I expect you'd like your family to be there?'

'Yes, I would. But I can't imagine they'll want to come.'

'Wouldn't you like your father to give you away?'

'I doubt if he will,' she said honestly. 'He won't be very happy.'

'No. I dare say that after Longton I'll come as something of a shock.'

Knowing there was no point in denying it, she said quietly, 'For one thing it's so sudden. There'll hardly be time to let them know.'

'I'll either phone or email them as soon as we get back to Harefield.'

'I think you'll be wasting your time.'

His voice like polished steel, he said, 'I'll get them there.' Then, with a quick, sidelong glance, 'But just at the moment I have something more important on my mind.'

Drawing into a lay-by shielded from the road by a stand of trees, he stopped and switched off the engine and the main beam.

Her heart began to race with suffocating speed as he unfastened both their seat belts and took her in his arms.

In the greenish glow from the dashboard she saw him smile. 'There's no need to look quite so apprehensive. It's a shade public to do much more than kiss you.'

He kissed her lightly, almost playfully, but when her lips parted beneath the gentle pressure of his he began to explore her mouth with a hungry passion that made her stomach clench and sent her heart racing.

When he finally lifted his head she was past thinking, and if he'd suggested making love exactly where they were she would have offered no resistance.

He must have known she was his for the taking but, true to his word, he drew back and reached to fasten first her seat belt and then his own. A moment later they were on their way again, without a single car having passed.

Shaken to the soul by that brief interlude, she wondered how it was that no other man had ever been able to move her in the way this man did. His briefest kiss could summon up a storm of emotion, his lightest touch make her burn for him.

He had such power over her that it would have been frightening if he hadn't loved her as much as she loved him. But he must do, otherwise he wouldn't have gone to so much trouble to marry her.

She felt a warm glow of pleasure and excitement just reminding herself that by this time tomorrow she would be his wife…

As they approached Harefield Farm, and the security lights flashed on, Loris was surprised to see a large country mansion, rather than the homely farmhouse she had been expecting.

It was a square building, dignified and gracious, with creeper-covered walls and long windows flanking a handsome front door.

But, thinking back, Jonathan had told her that his sister had married the son of a local landowner.

As he helped Loris out and collected her case, he explained, apparently reading her mind, 'David's parents died a couple of years back, so he and Jane run the estate now.'

Having led the way into a spacious hall and up the stairs, he opened a door to the left. 'Jane said if all went well she was putting you in here.'

It was a pleasant room, with black oak floorboards, well-polished antique furniture, and a log fire burning cheerfully in the grate. A modern *en suite* bathroom had been added.

'I'm next door.' Dropping her case on the bed, he went on, 'I've a few things to attend to before I come up, so I'll say goodnight now.'

When she lifted her face for his kiss, he shook his head regretfully, 'I'd better not. If I kiss you once I may not be able to tear myself away.'

Disappointed, she reached up, and with her index finger

traced the curve of his cheek and jaw and the cleft in his chin. 'Would that matter?' she asked softly.

'Woman, are you trying to tempt me?'

'Yes. I've a lot of catching up to do.'

He laughed softly. 'Well, as I can resist anything but temptation, I'll be back in about half an hour.'

A little shocked by her own boldness, she had decided against a nightie, and, her hair loose around her bare shoulders, she was lying watching the flickering flames when he returned.

He was freshly showered and shaved, and wearing a short towelling robe. Discarding it, he slid in beside her and nuzzled his face against her breasts. 'Mmm...you're all scented and sensuous, like a velvety summer night.'

His warm wet tongue coaxed a pink nipple into life, and with a little murmur of appreciation he drew it into his mouth.

Shivers of pleasure ran through her, which were intensified when his fingers found its twin. Just when she thought she could stand no more of such exquisite torment his free hand slid down her flat stomach and began to explore.

She gave a little gasp as all sensation was dragged downwards and started to build and spiral into a growing need. When, without conscious volition, she began to move against his hand, it was withdrawn.

She whispered his name pleadingly.

Raising his head, he kissed her lips and said softly, 'There's no need to rush things, my love. Taking it slowly can mean maximum enjoyment. It will give me pleasure to experiment a little, to find out what pleases you most, then I can make our wedding night truly memorable.'

His index finger had been moving almost imperceptibly,

and now it paused and applied a light pressure. 'Do you like that?'

A little moan was all the answer he needed.

When Loris awoke she was alone in the bed and daylight was slanting in between the heavy velvet curtains.

Instant remembrance brought a fresh flood of happiness, and she sighed blissfully. Last night had been made up of love, tenderness, passion and ecstasy and, like the icing on the cake, today was her wedding day.

It didn't matter that it was to be a quiet wedding with no frills; it didn't matter that neither of them had much money; it didn't matter that Jonathan had no job. The only thing that mattered was having his love...

There was a knock at the door and she called, 'Come in.'

A young maid came in, carrying a tray of coffee and toast, and put it down carefully on the bedside table before drawing back the curtains.

'Mrs Marchant asked me to say that she's sorry to disturb you, but it's almost eleven-fifteen.'

'Eleven-fifteen!' Loris exclaimed, pushing herself upright. 'I'll never be ready in time.'

'She said that when you've had your toast and coffee, she'll be along to give you a hand... Oh, and Mr Drummond said you're to be sure and eat something, as he doesn't want you fainting at the altar.'

With a little bob, the girl scurried out.

As soon as Loris had eaten a slice of toast and swallowed a cup of coffee, she laid out the suit she'd brought, found some stockings and a set of dainty undies, and hurried into the bathroom to shower and clean her teeth.

When she emerged a few minutes later Jane Marchant was waiting, dressed in an elegant navy suit and hat. On the bed there were several boxes of various sizes, and a lovely bouquet of scented spring flowers.

'I see you have a suit ready,' Jane observed. Then, a shade diffidently, 'But I wondered if you'd like to wear this.' Taking the lid off the largest box, she lifted out an exquisite ivory silk wedding dress. 'We're pretty much of a size, and though it's seven years old these classic styles don't really change.'

Loris swallowed, momentarily too full to speak.

Noting the hesitation, Jane said hastily, 'Please feel free to refuse if you don't want to. I promise I won't be offended.'

'I'd *love* to wear it.'

Her pleasure obvious, Jane helped Loris into the dress and fastened a row of tiny covered buttons that ran down the back from the neck to below the waist.

It fitted perfectly.

Looking at her reflection in the cheval-glass, Loris said huskily, 'It's *beautiful.*'

Jane beamed. 'The accessories are all here if you want them. Shoes, headdress, and this.' She produced a garter embroidered with blue forget-me-nots.

When Loris had eased the garter into place, she tried the shoes. Luck was with her, and they too fitted.

'Are you wearing your hair up or down?' Jane asked eagerly.

'Up, I think.'

When her chignon had been pinned into place, Loris found that the headdress, a simple rhinestone coronet that held a veil as fine as gossamer, sat as neatly as she could have wished.

'All ready, with five minutes to spare,' Jane said, handing Loris the bouquet, 'and you look absolutely gorgeous.'

'If I do, it's thanks to you...'

A knock at the door cut through her words.

'That'll be David,' Jane said. 'He's offered to escort you to the church, if that's all right by you?' Then, seriously, 'I can't tell you how pleased I am that you're marrying Jonathan. He's one of the best.' Her eyes full of tears, she hurried out, just as her husband came in.

Having looked Loris over appreciatively, he nodded his approval. 'You look absolutely beautiful. My brother-in-law's a very lucky man... All ready?'

'Yes.'

Offering her his arm, he said, 'Then let's get going. We've a Roller waiting.'

When he'd helped Loris into a ribbon-trimmed Rolls-Royce, they made the short drive in pale winter sunshine, to find the small church full of flowers, the village organist playing Bach, and a grey-haired priest waiting to welcome them.

A mere handful of people were present, amongst them her mother, who was seated in the front pew, and her father, who was standing at the back of the church.

To Loris's surprise, he took David's place, and walked her up the aisle, while Simon, clearly about to perform the duties of best man, waited at the chancel steps with Jonathan.

As she reached her bridegroom's side, he turned his head to smile at her.

Knowing he must have moved heaven and earth to get her family here, she returned his smile, her heart overflowing with love and gratitude.

The short service passed like a dream—the quietly spoken vows, the exchange of rings, her bridegroom, handsome and self-assured putting back her veil to kiss her, and finally the signing of the register.

In the vestry, looking unexpectedly tearful, her mother kissed her, and said, 'I hope you'll be happy.'

Her father, unsmiling and terse, added, 'I just hope you know what you're doing.'

Simon gave her a hug and wished her, 'The best of luck.'

Then a tall grey-haired man she had never seen before came up to take her hand and say, 'So you're Loris. My nephew has very good taste.'

Moments later they were out in the weak sunshine, and the local photographer was taking pictures.

'Time we were going to get changed,' Jonathan said in his bride's ear. 'Jane and David and Simon, who know what's going on, will take care of the reception and explain our absence.'

'Why are we leaving so soon?'

'We have a plane to catch, and we're cutting it rather fine.'

He took her hand and, showered with rice, they ran down the church path to the waiting Rolls.

By seven o'clock that evening they were in Paris, at the Hotel L'Epic, being shown into the luxurious honeymoon suite by the manager himself.

This was yet another surprise in a day full of surprises.

When Monsieur Duval had bowed himself out Jonathan opened the waiting champagne and poured them each a glass.

Watching Loris while she sipped, he asked, 'Tired?'

'A little,' she admitted. 'It must be the excitement.'

'Hungry yet?'

'Not really.' They had eaten a sandwich on the plane.

'So, shall we say dinner at eight-thirty?'

'Yes, fine.'

'Do you want to go downstairs? Or shall we have it sent up?'

'Oh, sent up, I think.' She had nothing suitable to wear for dinner in a first-class hotel.

Once again reading her mind, he said, 'As soon as the shops are open we'll go and buy you a trousseau.'

Knowing the honeymoon suite must be costing the earth, she said hurriedly, 'Oh, no, I don't need any new clothes.'

'As you've virtually nothing with you, if you don't buy *something* we'll have to spend the rest of our honeymoon in bed.' A glint in his eye, he added, 'Not that that's such a bad idea... But first, in order to keep up our strength, we'll need to eat, so is there anything special you'd like me to order?'

'No, I'll leave it to you.'

While he ordered the meal, in fluent French, she put her glass on the coffee-table and went to the window to look out over the Place Chaumont, a quiet square with wrought-iron lamps and elegant buildings.

The last eight hours had had an unreal, dreamlike quality that made her feel as if she wanted to pinch herself to make sure she was really awake.

Instead, she looked down at the plain gold band that Jonathan had slipped onto her finger. Everything had happened so quickly that there'd been no time to wonder if she'd done the right thing in marrying a man she scarcely knew.

Suppose she'd made a dreadful mistake? Suppose what she felt for him was just sexual attraction rather than love? Suddenly racked by doubts, she clasped her hands tightly together.

No, if what she felt for him wasn't love, then there was no such thing. Sexual attraction was there, certainly, but there was so much more—warmth and caring, a liking and respect for the kind of person he was, a deep and abiding need to be with him, to be a part of him...

So long as he felt those things too, their marriage would be a happy one... But *did* he? All at once she was beset by fresh doubts. He'd never once said he loved her...

Though surely he must do, otherwise why would he have bulldozed her into marrying him?

Replacing the phone, he came to stand behind her and kiss her nape, before turning her into his arms and covering her mouth with his.

His kiss was passionate and searching, a devastating mixture of possessiveness and desire that made her body tremble and her head spin, so that she was forced to cling to him.

Sweeping her into his arms, he crossed to the sumptuous couch and laid her on it. Then, sitting by her side, looking down at her, he said with undisguised triumph, 'Mine at last.'

'You sound as if you've waited for years,' she remarked huskily.

'I have. Almost as long as Jacob waited for Rachel.'

She thought for a second or two that he might be teasing her, but something about the way he spoke made her know he wasn't.

Suddenly, clearly, she recalled him talking about unrequited love, and saying, 'I wasn't good enough for her... However, that was a long time ago.'

Pushing herself up, so she was half lying back against the cushions, she said, 'You knew me in the past.' It was a statement, not a question. 'When?'

'You'd just started at the School of Art and I'd finished college and was working for your father. The minute I saw you I knew you were what I'd always wanted. I started going to Bohemian Nights—if you remember, it was where a lot of the art students went for coffee or a cheap pizza— and after weeks of worshipping from afar I plucked up enough courage to talk to you. When I discovered you liked the cinema, I asked you to come to the Carlton with me...'

'*Johnny*... Of course...' Though both had been shy there had been an instant affinity, and she'd thought he might be the someone special she'd been waiting for. 'Ever since I first saw you I've had the feeling that I once knew you...'

'But I was of so little account that you didn't even recognise me.'

'I half did. If you remember, at the party, I asked you if we'd ever met before, and you said no.'

He shook his head. 'I said, *"If we had, I would have remembered"*.'

'And you were angry that I didn't?'

'Let's say disappointed.'

'But it was years ago, and I only knew you for a very short time. You told me your name was Johnny Dudley, and you looked so completely *different* then. You were *boyish*... Diffident and unassuming...'

As though curious, he asked, 'Why did you agree to go out with me?'

'Because I wanted to.'

His voice cool, he pointed out, 'You didn't come.'

'I intended to, but it happened to be my father's birthday. He'd made arrangements to take some friends to Maxim's, and because their son was coming too he insisted on me going to even up the numbers. When I told him I had a date, and who with, he said if I wrote you a note he'd see you got it.'

'Can you remember what you said in the note?'

'I explained why I couldn't come, and suggested we met the following night at the same time and place. I asked you to phone me if you couldn't make it. I didn't hear from you, so I went to the Carlton and waited for over an hour.'

Jonathan's face looked so hard and set that her voice wavered as she continued, 'The next day I went into the offices, hoping to see you, but I was told you hadn't come in to work. A few days later, when I asked again, my father told me you'd left without a word. Why did you leave so suddenly?'

'I didn't exactly *leave*, I was thrown out.'

'Thrown out?'

'For getting too familiar with the boss's daughter.'

As Loris stared at him, aghast, he went on, 'Instead of giving me your note, your father gave me my marching orders. He said he didn't want one of his workforce "trying it on" with his daughter. Like a fool, I denied "trying it on", and admitted that I was serious and I wanted to marry you. He roared with laughter before pointing out that I was a nobody, with no money and no background. That I wasn't, and never would be, good enough to clean your shoes, let alone marry you, so I was wasting my time trying to date you. I told him you were of an age to make up your own mind, and that you'd already agreed to meet me that night. He said, "Don't think for a minute she'll turn up, boy. She's just been enjoying a bit of fun at your expense. Tonight she's having dinner at Maxim's with the son of Sir Denzyl Roberts". I didn't want to believe him. I waited outside Maxim's and saw your party arrive. You were escorted by a handsome fair-haired man. He had his arm around your waist.'

Taking a deep breath, she said, 'That was Nigel.'

Jonathan muttered something under his breath that might have been an oath, before saying, 'I hope your father was proud of himself.'

'To be honest, it was more likely to have been my mother's influence that made him act as he did. I don't think my father would have cared enough.'

'He cared enough not to want you to marry a penniless nobody. I would have given a lot to have seen his face when I first broke the news to him.'

Understanding at last why Jonathan had railroaded her into this marriage, Loris went icy cold, as if every drop of blood had drained from her body.

He hadn't married her because he loved her. It had been to settle old scores.

How many times had she said, 'I wish you'd be serious'? Now she knew he was, and had been from the start. Deadly serious.

She felt a crushing despair.

Slowly, she said, 'So that's why you were so determined to have my parents there, to savour your triumph. You hate them both.'

'Not at all,' he denied smoothly. 'Your mother can't help being the kind of person she is, and your father has actually done me a great service. If it hadn't been for him I might have lacked ambition. He gave me the incentive to get where I am today.'

'In a Paris hotel that neither of us can afford,' she said bitterly. 'Well, as far as I'm concerned you don't have to worry, because I'm leaving right now.'

When she tried to struggle up, he stopped her. 'I'm afraid I can't let you leave.'

'Why not? After all, you've done everything you set out to do. You've married the boss's daughter, and given your sister-in-law a chance to keep Mark. What else could you possibly want?'

'A lifetime with you.'

'I've no intention of staying with a man who doesn't love me. Who simply used me to get even with my father.'

'I admit that getting even with your father was part of it, but only a tiny part. I fell in love with you when you were eighteen, and I've never stopped loving you. For the past few years I've worked fourteen hours a day with one thing in mind. You. I hardly dared hope that when I got where I wanted to be you'd still be free. Luckily I was almost there when Jane told me about your engagement...'

Dazed by the rush of happiness, Loris said nothing.

Watching her bemused face, Jonathan asked quizzically, 'Don't you want to know where "there" is?'

She didn't really care. The only thing that mattered was that he loved her. But she said dreamily, 'If you want to tell me.'

'I think I'd better, so you won't keep worrying about how I'm going to pay the bill. I don't work for Cosby's; I own it.'

Thinking she'd misheard, she said, 'What did you say?'

'I own Cosby's,' he repeated patiently.

'Own it?' Her jaw dropped, 'Then why did you pretend to be Mr Grant's PA?'

'I wanted the takeover to go through before anyone found out who I was.'

'But after it went through why didn't you tell me?'

'I needed to see if you'd marry me thinking I had nothing. When you agreed, I knew you must love me.'

He leaned forward to kiss her.

She put her hands flat on his chest and held him off.

'Something wrong?'

'I want the answers to some questions before you kiss me.'

'You're a hard woman,' he complained. Seeing she wasn't about to relent, he agreed, 'Okay, shoot.'

'I take it my father doesn't know you're his boss?'

'In the end I had to point it out to him to get him to come to the wedding. Anything else?'

'Is your name really Drummond?'

'Yes.'

'Then why were you calling yourself Dudley when we first met?'

'My grandfather, a dictatorial old man, ruled the family with a rod of iron. Even when his two sons were grown up he tried to run their lives. His eldest son, my uncle Hugh, gave in to pressure and took the course Grandfather "suggested'' he took. But my father wanted to be a doctor, and, what was worse, a GP rather than a Harley Street specialist, which infuriated Grandfather. There was a blazing row and he accused his younger son of wanting to debase the name Drummond, and said if he didn't toe the line he could get out. My father left the ancestral home, and, deciding to cut all ties with the old man, changed his name to Dudley, his mother's maiden name.'

Suddenly putting two and two together, Loris said, 'So "Uncle Hugh" must be Sir Hugh Drummond, and the ancestral home Merriton Hall…'

'That's right.'

'But when my mother asked if you were related to Sir Hugh Drummond, you said—'

'Ah, but she went on to ask specifically if he was my father, and I said my father was a poor GP. Which was the truth. He never made any money, but he was loved and respected, and when he died from an infection he'd picked up from one of his patients the whole town turned out to mourn. Grandfather, who was a very old man by then, came to the funeral. It seems he'd regretted the rift for some time but had been too proud and stubborn to make the first move. Hugh had never married, so I was his only grandson. He begged me to change my name to Drummond, to carry on the family name, and promised that when Hugh died everything would come to me. I told him politely that I wasn't interested, whereupon he told me a great deal less politely that I was as pig-headed as my father. My mother, who oddly enough felt sorry for the old man, and thought it would be a shame to let the name die out, wanted me to do it, so in the end I agreed, to make her happy.'

A thought occurred to Loris, and she began, 'The tall grey-haired man in the vestry—'

'Was Hugh,' Jonathan confirmed. 'Any further questions?'

'One thing puzzles me,' she admitted. 'You've only been in the States a few years and I was wondering…' She hesitated.

'How I come to own a firm the size of Cosby's?'

'Yes.'

'Well, I had a flying start. Can you remember me telling you that my mother's parents owned a small business in Albany? Well, that was Cosby's. By the time I went to live in the States my maternal grandparents were on the point of retiring. I took over from them, and when there was a huge boom in electronic communications I was able to buy them out. As a result of luck and a lot of hard work business increased tenfold, and profits soared…'

'When did you decide to take over Bergman Longton?'

'That had been one of my goals since the day your father told me I'd never succeed in marrying the boss's daughter.'

'Well, in a way you haven't.'

He looked at her, his sea-green eyes quizzical. 'What exactly does that mean?'

Flatly, dispassionately, she said, 'It means I'm not Peter Bergman's daughter. My mother was already pregnant when she got married. She tried to pretend I was his, but he knew she was lying. In the end, to save looking a fool, he agreed to pass me off as his own. But I don't think he's ever really forgiven her, or me. My mother still doesn't know I know.'

'So how *do* you know?'

'Understandably, perhaps, the man I still call Father has never liked me, and one day when I'd particularly annoyed him he told me the truth. I was thirteen at the time.'

'It must have come as a shock.'

'In some ways it was a relief to know I wasn't his child.'

'That fact certainly explains a lot of things—why he didn't help you through college, why he left you to fend for yourself, why he didn't care overmuch about your happiness...'

'But a lot of good's come out of it,' she said quietly. 'It's because of him that I worked so hard to become a designer and be independent...'

A thought struck her, and she asked, 'You won't mind if I keep on working?'

'My love, you can work to your heart's content, though I'd like you to take Fenny Manor as one of your first assignments.'

'So it really is yours?'

'Ours. And when we eventually get back from our honeymoon we'll buy a nice place in town, for when we want to be in London.'

'Eventually? I thought we were only in Paris for a few days.'

'We're here for as long as you like, and after Paris I thought a trip to New York, to meet my mother and the rest of my family, then on to San Francisco, Hawaii maybe...'

'For someone who's a self-confessed home bird that sounds like pretty good going.'

Taking her in his arms, he held her close. 'You'll be travelling with me, and you know the old saying, "Home is where the heart is..."'

When he kissed her, in a haze of happiness she kissed him back, until kissing was no longer enough, and, on fire for him, she whispered, 'What time is it?'

'Eight-fifteen.'

'Oh...'

Hearing the disappointment in her voice, he left her for a moment to hang the 'Do not disturb' sign on the door. Then, taking her hand, he led her towards the bedroom.

Conscience stirring, she asked, 'What if they bring the meal?'

'They'll have the sense to leave it outside,' Jonathan said firmly. 'After all, this *is* France, and we *are* in the honey-moon suite.'

We're delighted to announce that

A Mediterranean Marriage

is taking place in

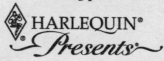

HARLEQUIN® Presents

This month, in THE BELLINI BRIDE by Michelle Reid, #2224

Marco Bellini has to choose a suitable wife.
Will he make an honest woman of his
beautiful mistress, Antonia?

In March you are invited to the wedding of
Rio Lombardi and Holly Samson
in THE ITALIAN'S WIFE by Lynne Graham, #2235

When Holly, a homeless young woman, collapses in front of
Rio Lombardi's limousine, he feels compelled to take her and
her baby son home with him. Holly can't believe it when Rio
lavishes her with food, clothes...and a wedding ring....

Harlequin Presents®
The world's bestselling romance series.
Seduction and passion guaranteed!

Available wherever Harlequin books are sold.

HARLEQUIN®
*M*akes any time special ®
Visit us at www.eHarlequin.com

HPJANMM

If you enjoyed what you just read,
then we've got an offer you can't resist!

Take 2 bestselling
love stories FREE!
Plus get a FREE surprise gift!

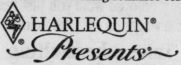

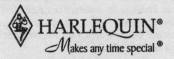

Coming Next Month

THE BEST HAS JUST GOTTEN BETTER!

#2229 THE CITY-GIRL BRIDE Penny Jordan
When elegant city girl Maggie Russell is caught in a country flood, rugged Finn Gordon comes to her rescue. He takes her to his farmhouse, laughs at her impractical designer clothes—and then removes them...piece by piece....

#2230 A RICH MAN'S TOUCH Anne Mather
The arrival of businessman Gabriel Webb in Rachel's life is about to change everything! She isn't prepared when he touches emotions in her that she has carefully hidden away. But is Gabriel interested in only a fleeting affair?

#2231 THE PROSPECTIVE WIFE Kim Lawrence
Matt's family are constantly trying to find him a wife, so he is instantly suspicious of blond, beautiful Kat. She's just as horrified to be suspected of being a prospective wife, but soon the talk of bedding and wedding starts to sound dangerously attractive—to both of them....

#2232 HIS MIRACLE BABY Kate Walker
Morgan didn't know why Ellie had left him. It was obvious she'd still been in love with him. But when he found her, to his shock, she had the most adorable baby girl he'd ever seen. Had Ellie found another man or was this baby Morgan's very own miracle?

#2233 SURRENDER TO THE SHEIKH Sharon Kendrick
The last thing Rose expected was to go on assignment to Prince Khalim's kingdom of Maraban. He treated her more like a princess than an employee. Rose knew she could never really be his princess—but their need for each other was so demanding....

#2234 BY MARRIAGE DIVIDED Lindsay Armstrong
Bryn Wallis chose Fleur as his assistant because marriage was definitely not on her agenda—and that suited him perfectly. The last thing he wanted was any romantic involvement. Only, soon he began to find Fleur irresistible....

HPCNM0102